Finding
Bertha

Finding *Bertha*

Linda Oberlin

LW Publishing

Author's Photographer	Lorenzo Gaspart
Book cover design	Christina Alta Luboski
Editing	Ginny Glass @ AZ Editing
Content design	Kimberly Martin @ Jera Publishing

ISBN 978-0-9911382-5-8

Published by

LW Publishing
Atlanta, Geogia, USA

To my brother, Ed

Acknowledgments

It is with enormous gratitude that I acknowledge the support and encouragement that has allowed me to write this story. I want to thank my children, Scott, Geoffrey, Lori, and my grandson, Elias. A special thank you to Mary and Lyndsay for having the courage to read the first draft and continue to cheer me on unconditionally. All have contributed greatly, and they are loved forever.

Preface

GROWING UP IN St. Louis, my grandmother and her sister were permanent fixtures in the lives of my family. At one point, they even lived with us. I can still picture them in their single beds, side by side, early in the morning, cups of tea—newspaper for Grandma and the Bible for Bertha. Bertha lived with my grandparents her whole life. After my grandfather died, the sisters never parted, not even in death—having strokes and dying within hours of each other in their 80's. Where Grandma went, Bertha followed. What Grandma ate; Bertha ate. If Bertha had been included in any decision making, her vote of family matters would have never deviated from that of my grandmother's vote. Bertha was always loved and respected by all members of the household. But she was considered odd and her religious interjections were simply tolerated regardless of their irrelevance to the subject at hand. She laughed when we laughed, but we were never quite sure if she ever really got the jokes.

As a little girl, Bertha had fallen ill to meningitis. Until the 20th century, the typical protocol for its treatment was either sulfonamides, or later, penicillin. Whether or not the disease was the source of her obvious disabilities throughout the remainder of her life was debated among the family for decades. However, there was no concrete evidence to explain her lifelong odd physical gate, loss of balance, and frequent falls.

Bertha was sweet, kind, and too often the casualty of our inside jokes. I loved her and found her demeanor a lovely calm respite from what would often be a loud boisterous family gathering. In my late teens, my grandmother and Bertha moved to Florida. My exposure to them grew infrequent and was minimized to a brief once a year visit. As my life progressed to dating, college, dorms, part-time jobs, etc. Bertha and Grandma continued as they had always done. They were happy, content, and together.

I got the news of my grandmother's death early one morning. I cried and was sad. Bertha had found her sister on the floor in the small kitchen area of their mobile home. She sought help from a neighbor who called for paramedics and watched helplessly as they whisked my grandmother to the hospital leaving Bertha behind. Family rushed to Grandma's side as she quickly slipped away due to complications of a massive stroke.

But approximately four hours after my grandmother died, I got the news that Bertha had died as well—in duplicate copy. When my cousin drove to the mobile home to collect Bertha and some of her belongs, he found her on the floor in the small kitchen area exactly as her sister had been found just hours before. Again, the paramedics rushed her to the same hospital, and within the hour Bertha succumbed to a massive stroke and passed away—just a few rooms down the hall from where her sister had died that same day. When I got the second call, I felt a deep and profound sadness. As if in life, Bertha had preferred to follow her sister's lead in death. The sweet, kind, calm, lovely little odd woman was gone.

Since her death, I've struggled with how I could have been a better force in her life, another outlet of communication, and love.

She always displayed great interest in me and inquired about my school, boyfriends, wedding plans, 1st baby with joyful enthusiasm. Had I shown her that I was interested in her life, as well, with enough reciprocal interest? Or did I just take it for granted that her life was just as it had always been, and further inquiry really wasn't necessary?

While attending Oglethorpe University, a professor had referenced the Kindertransport project within a classroom discussion. I knew little detail of the Kindertransport. I was aware of the 10,000 children rescued from Nazi Germany and paired with foster parents in England while most of their parents and families perished in various concentration camps throughout Europe, never to be reunited again. But I was unaware of some of the personal stories and details of that event and it compelled me to do more research of my own. Upon doing so, I read of the thousands of heroes who risked their own lives and those of their families to ensure the safety of as many children as possible. As well, I discovered some added names of warriors who persevered against Hitler's evil and brutal machine, only to find so many who had been murdered and tossed into heaps where millions of other bodies were simply stacked in piles in an ugly display of disregard for humanity. In an attempt to give some homage to those precious souls in this novel, I have included the real names and true accounts of Liselotte Herrmann, Fritz Rau and fellow students, Martha Wertheimer, Rabbi Leo Baeck, as well as artists and journalists who contributed greatly to documenting the stories through film, art, and journalism. They remain in our hearts as exemplary symbols of how true humanity can and does overcome, even at great sacrifice. It is my hope that I have represented their stories with honesty and dignity.

I began plotting out my historical fiction to spread the story of these amazing warriors and the journey of the brave parents and children caught in the horror. As well, the fictional characters I wanted to weave through the complex labyrinth of the war include my great aunt in name only. Although she remains a fictional character for the book it is my way of showing that her calm kindness and interest in my life was very real. And her unconditional love for me was more inspirational than she ever knew. Just as my character Bertha had done in this novel, my sweet great aunt nurtured a child and was part of a universal force that inspires us all to continue to protect and save our children in hopes of a kinder, safer, and more loving world.

1

To live is the rarest thing in the world.
Most people exist, that is all.
—Oscar Wilde

THE SHOCK OF the cold floor on my bare feet sent shooting pains through my shins. I was sore as hell from climbing up and down a ladder day after day. Over the past ten years, I had gained a portly forty-five pounds—mostly around the middle. I knew how it had happened: depression, divorce, the winter, losing my dad, and beer. Lots of beer.

The Northeast was experiencing one of the worst winters in five years. Although the storm of '96 was fierce, this little January surprise was a quick-moving snowstorm that managed to dump six inches by morning. The flakes stopped flying by around 8:00 a.m. Freezing gusts of wind blew through the cracks of the hundred-year-old house, making it impossible to keep warm. Adding a space heater and an electric blanket, I was able to curl up each night layered in flannel. I looked, felt, and probably smelled, like a warm plaid burrito.

Part of the heating system in the house was as old as the structure, and although the radiators still moaned, banged, and creaked, very little steam or heat escaped them. In the '80s, central heat had been added, but the ductwork looked like Swiss cheese, only to be connected to a gigantic, old, inefficient furnace. Everything in this house was old. And I was starting to feel old, too.

Meg wasn't awake yet, so I knew I had some time to sit on the edge of the bed to allow myself to acclimate to the world. She was still sleeping in my bed until I could figure out the heat situation. Her small frame looked even tinier in what she called "the big bed."

Tempted to return to my warm fetal position, I cursed under my breath and sprang up too quickly and headed to the bathroom. I take freezing weather personally—a total invasion of my life. My NYC friends kept referring to the light dusting of snow over Christmas as "beautiful" and "romantic." Not me. Winter just seemed to make everything more difficult, and I was looking forward to the end of it all.

I was shivering so hard that I struggled to get to the bathroom in time. And I was on a mission today. I only got Meg every other weekend. I had been petrified the first weekend alone with her. But with Meg's help, we managed just fine. At "four and three-quarters," she was the smartest person I knew. And the most charming. She was an old soul. She saw and got things that most adults missed. And she appeared to get me—more than her mother ever had. Meg quickly recognized I needed a lot of help. I was constantly rattling around in this large wooden space that echoed with every step. The overload of projects all at once kicked my ADD into overdrive. Misplaced tools, forgotten mail, and absence of time were the proof. I frequently felt like a small flounder that had just been jerked onto a large ship deck, flopping around in a panic. Having Meg here seemed to help me relax and prioritize. With her as the focus, I could put a lot on the back burner and just relax for a weekend.

Patiently, she offered instructions of her care, down to the very last detail. Bread was to be cut in triangles with no crust. Orange juice was not to have pulp, better known as "that stringy, yucky stuff." And before we dug in, the favorite purple plastic butterfly was clipped in the front of her wild, red, curly hair. With a few basic strategies in place, we happily ate, slept, dressed, and played together on our own, all without the intervening tensions of what had been a marriage of power struggles.

My attempt to acclimate to the world was taking much longer for me today. Last night had been a ball buster. Since inheriting the old house from Great-Aunt Bertha, I found myself totally engulfed in cleaning, gutting, repairing, painting, flooring, and rebuilding. I hadn't gotten to bed until well after midnight. I was half sick with exhaustion, but I knew that I had to persevere to make the space at least livable for Meg's weekend visits. Natalie, her mother, would certainly critique and censor my slightest moves, citing any lingering smell of cat piss, not to mention the occasional sighting of rat-shit pellets. Small pieces of cat food kicked under floorboards and hidden from sight were easily found by mice and rats. Small prehistoric skeletons were indications that the pesticide service was working. But with Natalie's control issues and critical eye, I couldn't take any chances. Any opportunity to blast me was fair game since I blamed her father's consistent interference in our lives for the ultimate death of our eight-year marriage. It didn't help that I referred to him at the divorce proceedings as the "nosy old bastard." For Meg's sake, and the fear of losing any visitation rights, I walked on eggshells around Natalie and remained in compliance with her every stupid whim. I had to admit, though, that Natalie was just the fire under my belt that helped me deal with an old house that no one in the rest of the family even wanted to consider.

Since the divorce in '98, Natalie had moved further away from New York City to be near her family in the small rural town of Chester. Although New Jersey certainly has a beautiful countryside that had earned its name as the Garden State, I just never pictured myself any further away from the city. I enjoyed loud mix of eateries, friends, and the local neighborhood bars within walking distance. But being an out-of-work carpenter in an economy that was headed for a hard recession was challenging at best. I would never be able to buy in NYC, and the only rent I could afford placed me in dangerous and compromised housing projects. I knew I would need some place to live that would accommodate Meg in a safe environment and close enough to ensure frequent visits. And I couldn't help but want to prove to my ex, and the nosy old bastard, that I was perfectly capable of creating a safe and loving home that any *normal* woman would crave. But the most important reason was for Meg. Hands down, the rest of them could go fuck themselves.

So I embraced the old structure with open arms, grateful that my aunt had left it up for grabs in what appeared to be the perfect timing of her death. It wasn't really a shock to anyone in the family. She had never married and, for years, rattled around in the large house alone. She appeared happy, content, and always smiling. But in later years, she had become somewhat immobile and dependent on a walker. Dad moved her bedroom downstairs, leaving the second floor vacant. And it showed. Her only source of companionship appeared to be a myriad of cats and the rotating parade of nursing attendants. Only the cats made periodic visits to the second floor.

Bertha was my great-aunt, the sister of my dad's mom, Freida. The most recent photo I remember of her was at Dad's graduation from Rutgers, class of '60. But I cruelly suspected that at ninety-seven years old, she appeared just as I had always remembered her anyway. As a child, I was somewhat uncomfortable around her. She chatted away and laughed at almost everything she said. I never really understood any of it. She spoke some Yiddish, mixed with English and German that was grammatically pitted. She was a small German Jew who had appeared matronly even in her youth. Old black-and-white photos of her revealed an odd haunting of a figure that leaned to one side, as if the only thing supporting her was a steady wind. She wore thin cotton dresses with tiny floral print and heavy leather oxfords that laced up the front. Her thick calves sank directly into the shoes with what appeared to be the absence of ankles. Her hair was black and carelessly pinned back in a loose bun. She wore a small gold Star of David that dangled on a long chain around her neck. On her wrist was an ornate watch that she frequently checked and adjusted. Those two pieces were the only jewelry I ever saw her wear, and she wore them every day.

As a young kid, I went to her house with Dad all the time. I enjoyed playing with the cats and any new kittens on the large wrap-around front porch. And Bertha always treated me to fresh baked cookies. I liked her and liked those visits. As I got older, however, so did she. She developed an unstable stomp as she walked toward me with open arms, ready to hug, and her lips were always wet. At one point, I had grown tall enough that we were face-to-face and the encounters became more difficult and dangerous to maneuver. With a lowered head, I stretched out my arms for a distant hug as she came in for the kill. I turned my head to the right and offered my cheek. With a spasmodic jerk, she struggled to meet her lips with my cheek and instead caught me on the mouth. The trauma of it was never forgotten, and I simply started waving from a distance.

My parents were good to Bertha and always helped when needed, without hesitation or complaint. Although my father, a man of few words, didn't ever really say much about Bertha, I did notice that he was typically the one who catered to her every need. She would hug him longer than anyone else. While rubbing and patting his back I could hear her hum in his ear and whisper, "Mayn yingele." *My little boy.*

In 1999, neighbors became suspicious that something was wrong. The small empty dish on the front porch and a few newspapers piled at the door were clues that the house was too quiet. Someone called 911. Bertha was found on the kitchen floor. A cold piece of toast remained on the counter, teeming with ants. Shortly after her body was discovered, my father was called. He hung up the phone, stared at the floor, and said, "I have to go to the house." Bertha's funeral was the only time I ever saw my father cry. A year later, we would bury him as well. His heart attack came on quickly while walking out to the mailbox one morning. He managed to make it back to the house, but once seated, he slumped forward at the kitchen table and died in the ambulance before reaching the hospital. He was laid to rest next to Bertha and my grandfather, Carl, in a small family plot in Grayson.

Throughout the following year, I stumbled through life in a virtual muddy murk. I was starting to feel like the last time I had felt any real joy was 1997—Meg's birth. Although the marriage had started showing stress fractures from the beginning, we blamed our lack of communication, greatly diminished sex, and frequent arguments on the *seven-year-itch* theory. Natalie wanted a child, so we decided to make one, thinking the sex and baby shopping would bring some romance back into our lives. It worked a little, for a while. But by Meg's first birthday it became painfully clear that we had fallen right back into the same bad habits and struggles.

So, in 2001, I accepted the challenge of my inheritance, sight unseen. I hadn't been inside the house for years, and it had been vacant since Bertha's death. I knew I had my work cut out for me. But I was in a bit of a bind financially, and the old house was in East Grayson, about ten miles from Chester, which was in perfect proximity to Meg but still a cushy distance from Natalie and her meddling family. Although I knew why no one else wanted it, I was ready for the challenge. A change in my life, a new focus, and a safe haven from the recession was exactly what I needed. Being near Meg was the bonus.

I stepped into a half-finished bathroom. Although the bare wood walls were a skeletal shell exposing more hidden sins than I cared to see at first light, I was beginning to see progress with the installation of a new toilet and a temporary metal shower. Relieving myself, I shivered and groaned contemplating what it was going to be like to try to piss as an old man. If I was this miserable at thirty-four, how would I ever endure living to eighty? An antique oval mirror hung precariously over the toilet. It had been part of the dark, Gothic, décor my aunt had preferred. Though it wasn't my taste, I was grateful for anything free. I focused on the yellow stream into the bowl for what seemed like an eternity, making sure not to spray the surrounding area from shivering.

As my eyes slowly made their way up to the mirror, I gasped. *My God! How old am I?* My hair was longer than usual and appeared to have been pushed up one side of my head as if I had skidded into bed the night before. I noticed a wiry gray hair springing out just above my right ear. I had a full mustache and beard peppered with the beginnings of gray. I had let myself go. I could blame the house. But the reality was that it had started toward the end of my marriage. Natalie always complained that I didn't take enough time with my appearance. She would buy clothes for me, and what she described as a "GQ look" only made me feel like a ridiculous little kid incapable of matching my shirts to my pants. Most of the garb she chose was not conducive to my career as a carpenter. So on the rare occasion we'd join friends on a night out, my clothes felt like a pretentious costume. I indulged her requests knowing that her family's disappointment in her marriage to a struggling self-employed carpenter was only more added pressure to our relationship.

With no real encouragement for Natalie to pursue a career, her father frequently reminded me that I was "the man of the house" when beginning conversations of house hunting, child rearing, and so on. I found his opinions archaic and inappropriately misogynistic. I found the lack of support and encouragement to Natalie sadly detrimental to her own welfare. Coming from a background of two educated working parents, I couldn't ever imagine raising my daughter to be anything other than independent. I tried to encourage Natalie, but rarely received a positive reaction. Therefore, with Natalie, I learned to pick my battles carefully. I compromised by spending more than necessary on the better haircuts and kept a tidy beard and mustache clipped short into a goatee. I had started growing my facial hair in high school. It helped to cover a slight indented scar that remained from corrective surgery I had received as a baby. Twentieth-century medicine proved successful in correcting cleft palates. But the echo of the kids' jokes on the playground created a scar deeper than the eye could see and imbedded years of insecurity. So I preferred the hairy mask.

Eli Henich
Took a sip
Drooled on down his gross hair lip!

Or my personal favorite:

Hair lip, hair lip
Tried to grin
Slobber dribbled
Down his chin!

"Children can be cruel, Eli," my mother repeated daily. "Forget about those nasty boys. And remember: you're the smart one!" Although that was all well and fine, basically what I heard was that I was a hideous-looking smart kid. I was small and named Elijah Paul Henich, of Jewish ancestry with a hair lip living in an Italian neighborhood. Thankfully, Dad had the insight to put a hammer in my hand. We didn't talk much save the occasional "Hold it like this, Eli," or, "Careful, son. Don't forget your protective eyewear." He probably never knew how I really felt out there or what was really going on in my head. But then again, I never really knew how he felt or what was going on in his head. He was quiet, deliberate, soft spoken, and calm—always calm. For me, his silence was necessary. Sometimes, he would toss in a line or two of some thought, inspiration, or just his outer monologue. Once he said, "There's a difference between moving on and moving forward. Sometimes, you can't move on as it means you leave behind something that is important to you. Instead, move forward. Take your valuables with you."

Time in the garage was my favorite with Dad. It became my sanctuary. Sundays were reserved for us. Mom only interrupted when bringing a snack or drink. Every Sunday, Dad and I had warm pretzels and beer. When I was little, my mug was filled with lemonade. With a big smile, Dad leaned forward and clicked our mugs together.

"Cheers," he said with a laugh.

On my sixteenth birthday, I was allowed the celebratory mug of beer. I don't know who was more proud. We clicked our mugs, hollered *cheers*, and laughed throughout the day. I never had the heart to tell him that my friends and I had partaken frequently in the clubhouse out back. But it was a special moment for us, nonetheless.

Although the intent was to keep me busy and settle my brain, the hammer became my weapon of choice, a weapon that allowed me to beat out my frustrations and nail my opponents, so to speak. With each creation, I envisioned pounding some dumb-ass kid in the head. *See? See what I made! Can you do that, asshole?* Eventually, thoughts of the assholes left me, and my hammering became more focused. When I was young, my building and construction started out small. Birdhouses and a wall rack for my baseball bats were the perfect project for the small, inexperienced hands of a kid. They only required a couple of boards and could typically be completed in an afternoon. As I grew, my projects grew. Dad taught me how to use the necessary tools for the more complex building. Christmas 1987, my pride and love for carpentry soared when I built a blanket chest for Mom as a gift. Equipped with a removable inside tray for small trinkets, a piano hinge with a friction support arm to save fingers from a slamming lid, and a simple carved-rose embellishment on the face of the chest brought loud cheers from the family and teary eyes from Mom as they all marveled at my craftsmanship. To a gawky fourteen-year-old boy with a scarred lip, it was a defining moment, and a carpenter was born.

Over time, my murderous hobby evolved into a lucrative career. During the building boom of the mid-'90s, I was able to put away some serious cash. Hours alone in a garage enabled me to perfect my craft. It was the one quiet space where I could really get away. But while I honed in on my skills, the solitude did nothing for the low self-esteem and the shyness that shadowed me into manhood. Gently, Dad would whisper, "Breathe in and breathe out, Eli."

Gazing into Bertha's mirror, I wondered where that small boy had gone. I stared at my face in disbelief of my own sleepless sallow appearance and realized how hard I'd been on that fresh-faced kid with the small scar. Looking at the large scruffy monstrosity before me allowed me to remember myself with much kinder eyes.

My trip down memory lane and my focus was broken as I heard Meg's little slippers scuffing across the old wooden floors toward the bathroom. I quickly closed my robe and ran my fingers through my matted mass of hair in hopes of presenting a much more handsome father figure to the only person I would probably ever really love. I exited the bathroom and turned the corner into the bedroom where she stood. Looking up at me, she was a little doll. Her hair, like mine, also looked as though she had skidded into bed. It was uncanny how it looked so beautiful on her and yet so ridiculously cornball on me. I scooped her up and cupped my hand around her small pink cheeks. I marveled at her face. After waiting nine very long intense months through Natalie's pregnancy, I was relieved and grateful for my beautiful baby. Her flawless skin and tiny rosebud lips took my breath away and she was perfect.

"Good morning," I quacked in my best duck impersonation.

"Daddy! You don't do it right!" She giggled. "I'm hungry."

The kitchen was old fashioned. But it was spotlessly clean. I put my attention to that area of the house first. We needed a sanitary place to eat. The cabinets were white metal with black hardware and hinges, all of which made it easy to gut and wash down with disinfectant. I scoured the tile countertops and linoleum floors free of critter residue. The couple of indoor cats left behind after Bertha's death had been fostered out to caring neighbors. Without the daily free handouts on the porch, the remaining outdoor feral crowd had long disappeared. The frilly curtains and crocheted toaster cozies were the first to go as well. I sanded down the oak kitchen table and chairs to the bare blond wood and coated them with three protective layers of polyurethane. By Natalie's standards, my kitchen would never be considered up-scaled, modern or chic. But remodeling a kitchen was just a budgetary impossibility and would have to wait. Besides, Meg had once said she liked it because it looked like Goldilocks's house. That was a compliment. I had read that book to her every night while vacationing at the lake one summer. She never got tired of it, and it became *our* book. Now, it was *our* kitchen.

Meg sat in a chair at the table wedged in the corner. Her throne allowed her to watch me cook, make coffee, clean up dishes, and stumble around in my desperate mission for caffeine. At the same time, she could watch the squirrels, birds, or any other act of nature out the large window. Today, however, animals were few and far between as they took shelter from the bitter cold and wind. Sitting near the window, Meg was a vision. The gray-and-blue hues of crystalized frost on the glass bounced off her ivory skin. As she delicately picked at her toast, I marveled at how something so small could appear to stop all anxieties and fears that typically encircled in my brain.

My vibrating cell phone startled me as it danced across a small metal counter. Somewhere it was buried in a neglected corner section of the counter that became a dumping ground for unpaid bills, expired coupons, and a few nuts and bolts whose origins I couldn't identify. I quickly dug down and grabbed up the phone to end the annoying buzz. I rarely heard from friends anymore since I had moved from the city.

We were all busy with our separate lives on completely different islands. I wasn't surprised to see Mom's name on the phone as there was only one person that would be calling me so early on a Saturday morning.

"Hello, Mother," I said cheerfully. "Yes, Mom, it's me. You called my cell phone. Who else could it be? Sorry, I'm a little sarcastic before coffee. I'm ok. I was just up very late working on the house. I got the toilet working upstairs, and I can take a shower now—that's a plus!"

I had to cut her off. "Mother, Meg is here. Can I call you back? I'm sorry. Her hands are kind of sticky from breakfast. I'll have her call you back. Mom?....Mom?...Yes, buying the paint today. Mother?... Mom!...I have to go; my breakfast is burning!"

I hated being abrupt with her. I've worried that she might be lonely since Dad passed away last year. She loves to talk on the phone and has taken a personal interest in my house, in a decorative kind of way. At some point, I'll call upon her expertise for Meg's room. Also, she frequently brings up stories about Bertha and the house. Lately, I have heard more stories about Great-Aunt Bertha's cats and the family than I really care to hear about since moving in, none of which are very interesting or exciting. As I've gotten older my curiosity of the ancestral tree has grown. Unfortunately, no one has offered up anything worth noting, birthplace, birthdate, number of siblings, and so on. Really nothing more than what a census could provide.

My grandmother Freida occasionally brought up an uncle that supposedly was from Alsace, France, whose career was of questionable acceptance. She consistently whispered *actor* when debating his rightful lineage to the family. Evidently, being Jewish or French is one thing, but never an *actor*! At this point, I guess I would rather create and build beautiful furniture and spaces than spend my time building a family tree. Besides, I would be a little afraid of what I would find when digging into the lives of my ancestors. I'm not that fond of the ones that are still here. Hopefully, someday I will get news that I'm actually related to somebody super fun, like Doc Holliday or Rasputin.

My coffee was getting cold, and I was anxious to sit with the paper and Meg for a few minutes before jumping into the day. I made my way through the house and opened the heavy front door. Still in my robe, I could stretch, grab up the paper, and still be half in and half out of my house. This morning, half was way better than whole. Just as I extended my one arm toward the damp frozen paper while hanging on for dear life to the doorjamb with the other hand, I glanced up to see a young woman across the street. She was in the doorway of the house directly across from mine. In an odd Fellini sort of way, our actions were perfectly mirrored. I was so entranced by this that I paused just long enough for her to glance up. In that moment, we were suspended in time, gazing across the street, both in robes, contorting our bodies for a paper. She beamed a broad smile and waved. In one fluid motion, I gave a quick wave with the free hand, swooped up the paper, and darted into the house behind the door. Regardless of the robe, I still felt as though I had been caught naked. Frozen, I stood there peering through the glass.

"I want more juice, Daddy!"

I hurried back to the kitchen, poured her juice, and sat down. Mindlessly, I scanned through the pages of news while Meg and I talked about her more important issues of the day: squirrels, toast, coloring books, and puppets.

"Meg, I think it's time we paint your room. Would you like to go to the paint store and choose the color?" I offered.

She immediately sat straight up, giggled, and clapped. As far as I was concerned, Meg had final say for her room. I wanted her to feel she always had a sanctuary where she could create, dream, and imagine. I knew that, once I got the color right, Mom would help her pick out the rest. Mom was good at *theme* rooms. When I was seven, she had created my room around the solar system. I helped her paint the walls and ceiling a midnight blue. I loved spending time stretched out on my bed and gazing at all the small plastic stars, moons, and planets she had glued to the ceiling. At night, after light had charged them throughout the day, they glowed in the dark. The few trusted friends I invited over thought my room was cool. I knew Mom was the perfect candidate to help Meg create her perfect room. It was a way to get Mom involved in a project she would love for a granddaughter she cherished.

Meg rode high on my shoulders as we climbed the steps and into her room. For now, it was barren with the exception of a single sleigh bed, small dresser, and nightstand. The walls were dingy and pale, but the plaster was in good shape. Paint would help. Opposite the wall of windows were two large closets. Meg wouldn't need both for clothes. Instead, I decided to convert one of them into a desk with shelving. For Meg, it could provide an area where her creativity could take flight at any given moment. Once completed, I could put bins of crayons, watercolors, markers, pencils, stickers, and glue sticks, on the shelves. She loved to color, draw, and make little books that she shared with friends and family. I stashed a few of my favorites away in my file cabinet. Personally, I felt many of them were worth publishing.

I let her pick out the clothes from her backpack and helped her with the tiny buttons on her little green shirt. She slipped on her jeans that had a permanent cuff at the ankle. I marveled at how small the stitching was and wondered if her clothes had been made by elves. She showed me how she liked her socks rolled down around her ankles and then she slipped on her sneakers. She allowed me to tie them for her. I wasn't good with little girls' hair, so I left it in ringlets and allowed nature to take its course. She was perfect.

I showered quickly and threw on clean work clothes. Off we went on an adventure that would include paint, brushes, rollers, pans, and of course, cheese pizza. I felt energy come back in my body and my mood lighten. I was excited about completing this room—Meg's room—in our house.

2

I think I've discovered the secret of life…
you just hang around until you get used to it.
—Charles M. Schulz

"WELCOME, EVERYONE! IF I may have your attention, please. Thank you all so much for coming to this year's very first meeting of Friends of East Grayson! Many years ago, my ancestors began their journey across torturous seas. Seeking refuge on our teeming shores, they…"

The minute Juanita Paulson started talking, I regretted my decision to attend. Her voice was grating and pretentious. Earlier, she'd do-si-doed through the room, weaving a web of hugging and patting. She was loud in volume and desperate for attention. Her voice was a chasm of trilled *R*s, overextended vowels, and just mindless chatter. She had secured her rightful place with the Daughters of the Revolution by claiming her direct lineage to the Mayflower and Thomas Jefferson. She took it upon herself to step up as the leader of the pack, and no one appeared to have the energy to dispute her position. Juanita had command of the stage, and she wasn't going to end it anytime soon. And my attention deficit wouldn't tolerate it for long.

A little depression set in after sending Meg back home for the next two weeks, and I found myself dealing with it in my usual manner. Barricaded in the house, I justified my actions with necessary house repairs. Our weekend together was perfect, and I missed her immediately after dropping her off with Natalie at the usual midway meeting spot. Natalie and I compromised by exchanging our child at a strip mall between East Grayson and Chester. It always felt like a dirty money laundering encounter. Although we agreed it would be a mutual accommodation allowing us to act like *grown-up adults* in front of our daughter, the reality was that neither of us really wanted to be in each other's house. Mom rode with me this time so we could stop for lunch together on the way back to East Grayson. She sensed my somber mood and knew my pattern of occasional self-isolation. Over lunch, she convinced me to attend the meeting. I had made the grave mistake of telling her about the invitation I'd found stuck in the welcome basket left on my front porch. She insisted that it would be a great way to meet the neighbors, make new friends, and learn the local merchants. She was right. Meeting more people could lead to some contract jobs and better deals during my renovation of the house.

"And a girl, perhaps?" She smiled. I ignored the question. Not ready for that yet—or ever. I'm a thirty-seven-year-old single father living in an old litter box. Dating was the last thing on my mind. I don't date "girls," and I won't discuss women with my mother. Not totally convinced, I took her advice and attended the meeting.

At last, Juanita reluctantly handed the mic over to some old guy. His soft voice and monotone speech about the road projects, painting the library, and the benefits of pine straw sent my mind into escape mode. I scoped out the potential for a nearby exit that could be swift and covert. His voice faded as I allowed my thoughts to drift back to earlier in the day.

I'd woken up early that morning on a mission to tackle Meg's closet. I had a full two weeks before seeing her again, and I wanted to surprise her with the built-in art center. At the paint store, she had chosen a pale purple, and she was excited to get started. I knew she would get tired before we finished, so I knocked out the rest of it on the first night she was gone. With the walls done, I was inspired to keep going. The closet, although tall and wide, had a shallow depth. I really couldn't do anything to deepen it as it would cut into the existing plumbing in the wall. My limited funds restricted me from rerouting pipes. I squeezed myself into the existing space and started sanding the floor. As I inched my way backward from one end to the other, I misjudged the distance of the length and put my boot through the wall behind me. *Fuck*! Damaging the wall was just another delayed moment because of my impatience and carelessness. I cut off the switch to the hand sander, crawled forward, and turned out of the closet on hands and knees. I rocked back and briefly sat on my ass and stared at the floor while trying to catch my breath. *Breathe in, breathe out.* "Bring it down, Eli," I could hear Dad say. "You will accomplish a lot more if you just bring your emotions down a notch."

I got my composure in check, leaned forward into the closet, and stared at what I thought was going to be a big hole. Instead, there was a small odd portal equipped with hinges and a latch. My boot had simply pushed open the door that had been hidden under layers of old paint. After years of renovating old homes, I was aware that many of them had small hidden spaces where people attempted to hide their stuff. Sometimes it was money or bonds. But mostly, it was just crap found a hundred years or so later. Once, I had found old whiskey bottles under the eave in a root cellar, an obvious attempt to hide a *disgusting habit* from somebody's old lady.

My curiosity was piqued. As I unhooked my utility light from above, I gingerly inched the light into the portal. I tapped the floor as I made my way closer, as not to come face-to-face with something furry. It was about a foot deep, and the flooring was level with the closet. What looked like an old swatch of carpet lay at the bottom. I peeled up one corner, and it easily lifted as I pulled it out of the hole.

It was a single piece of paper, dusty and yellowed with age. I couldn't really see what it was, so I scooted backward out of the closet again for closer inspection. Immediately, I felt a pang of disappointment. It was just an old newspaper. You hear about people finding bundles of money, sometimes in the millions, strapped to the back of an old donated piano or neatly stacked under floor boards. Not me. Nope. No such luck. I flung it out onto the floor and continued sanding.

Later, I headed to the kitchen for more coffee and grabbed up the paper. I was about to pitch it in the trash when I noticed it was dated 1927. Written in German, it was an issue of the *Die Rote Fahne*. All through school I loved history, especially when the stories were shocking. It never ceased to amaze me that truth was, indeed, stranger than fiction. My eyes scanned the page. I had never learned the language, save a few curse words uttered by my grandfather, Carl. However, the name Bertha Plesser jumped off the page and smacked me in my dumbfounded face. Although I couldn't translate what I was looking at, *von Bertha Plesser* was clearly printed as the writer of an article. After a few attempts to pull out some familiar words, I realized I couldn't decipher enough to understand the significance. I carefully placed the paper on the side table in the hall, and I couldn't stop thinking about it. Finding Bertha's paper, discovering a portal, and not damaging the wall gave me a new surge of energy and happiness.

While sitting in the meeting, my mind continued to obsess on the paper and the unknown text Bertha had written. I wasn't aware of how much time had passed. Juanita was talking again. Not paying attention, I hadn't a clue what she had been talking about and really didn't care. But great relief, and exhaustion, came over me when I heard the words *fresh baked cookies*. The meeting was finally ending, and I saw an opportunity to break loose out the back door. It was past my happy hour, and I needed a beer.

I quickly stood up, spun around, and smacked into a petite body standing directly in my path. The stack of pamphlets in her hands flew into every direction and across the floor. Naturally, all eyes swished toward me, and a screaming hush grew over the crowd.

"I am so very sorry," she whispered as she stooped down to pick up the mess.

"N-no, it was my fault," I stammered.

I bent down on one knee and began picking up my share. Embarrassed by the uncomfortable proximity, I immediately ducked my head and snatched up brochures at a furious pace to keep myself busy.

"Oh! You're the nephew that moved into Bertie's house!"

She had made her way closer to me. She was practically beaming in my face. She had the most beautiful set of teeth I'd ever seen. Stunned, I just nodded. At that moment, I realized that she was the woman I had seen across the street, the one who'd seen me half naked. I recognized her mop of curly blond hair and broad smile. Closer, I could see she had large blue eyes with flecks gold. Or were they just reflecting light off the carpet? I caught myself gawking at her and abruptly stood up. She bounced up, and I handed her my collected share of brochures.

"I'm happy to finally meet you. I'm Penny," she continued. "We're neighbors…across the street. I heard you had moved in. I loved Bertie. I'm sorry for your loss."

I wasn't surprised at how quickly word had buzzed about in a small town. But Mom was the only one I had ever heard call her Bertie. It felt odd to hear it from a stranger.

"I teach at East Grayson Middle School. Borrowing some travel brochures for a project with my kids." She leaned in and whispered, "Or should I say I'm stealing?"

She laughed out loud. Penny was gregarious and personable. There was something about her that made me want to stay. But I didn't have much to talk about. I had spent the past few months alone except for the weekend visits with Meg and occasional dinners with Mom. I was losing the art of conversation, and it was obvious.

"Goodbye, see you all next month," Juanita called out from across the room, confirming the end of the Friends of East Grayson's very first meeting of the year. Together, Penny and I headed toward the door. But the foot traffic created a wedge between us, and we were separated. Her arm popped above the sea of heads and waved. "See you again soon, Eli!" I found myself trying to keep track of her going out the door, but eventually, her small frame disappeared into the crowd.

I kicked off my shoes at the front door and headed for the fridge. Thankfully, there was one beer left in the door, and I didn't have to share. I screwed off the cap and flipped it into the trash as I swiftly walked out of the kitchen and into the hall. The newspaper was where I had placed it earlier in the day—the old credenza by the front door. I threw down my keys and grabbed it and swerved into the room that was most probably the parlor at some point in history but now housed my tools and table saw. This led me out to the deck where I could plop down.

Since my family had a "rich German-Jew heritage," as Mom frequently reminded me, they had been hopeful I would take German, Latin, or even Hebrew while in college. I didn't. I had absolutely no desire to speak any other language save English. However, I did sign up for French briefly. All the pretty girls took French, the romance language. Little did I know that I would be stuck and isolated in a cubicle of a language lab with headphones and a microphone repeating phrases of how to find a library or the appropriate way to borrow a pencil. I rarely saw any girls. I withdrew that semester.

Again, my eyes scanned the paper to confirm the date: 1927. The date was mind-boggling to me. *What was Bertha doing writing for a German newspaper in Berlin right before WWII? And where was her sister, Freida, my grandmother?* It became increasingly clear I knew very little about my grandparents and Great-Aunt Bertha.

The beer was cold, and I immediately chugged half the bottle. My eyes were starting to swirl from exhaustion. As I swigged the last of the beer, I felt my body take a slump that felt more like a plunge. I was more tired than normal. It was still early in the evening, but I felt comfortable about heading for bed knowing I had accomplished quite a bit throughout the day. I carefully placed the newspaper back on the hall table and climbed the stairs. My legs struggled with each heavy step.

As I sat on the edge of my bed, I flopped backward onto an unmade mess. I laid there staring at the ceiling and thinking about Meg. She was back with her mother and I missed her already. But admittedly, I was grateful I could sleep in tomorrow. I tried to make a mental note and list of tomorrow's chores but found myself continuously drifting back…drifting back to earlier in the evening…an annoying meeting…Juanita's painful voice…Bertha…the newspaper… my neighbor…her smile…

3

What and how had I lost by trying to do only what was
expected of me instead of what I myself had wished to do?
—Ralph Ellison, *Invisible Man*

"HI, DADDY!" SHE sounded so tiny on the phone.
"Hi, baby!" I tried to sound cheerful. I knew I
wouldn't see Meg this weekend. We were deviating
from the regular routine in preparation for the coming school year.
Winter, spring, summer—it all flew by, and my baby was growing
way too quickly. In the spring, Meg celebrated her fifth birthday.
Of course, Natalie controlled the event with an elaborate party at
her parent's house. Basically, the only friend I knew in the room
was my daughter, and she was totally inundated with thirty other
children and an outdoor mini circus. Eventually, I dropped my
gift on the table, hugged Meg, and left. Mom and I celebrated
Meg's birthday the following weekend at East Grayson's favorite
pizza parlor, some balloons, and Mom's homemade cupcakes. Mom
bought her a beautiful doll and a nice collection of books. I bought
her a bracelet with little silver animals that dangled as charms. As
well, I got her a journal—my mother's suggestion. Meg appeared
to be delighted with her gifts, and as I tucked her into bed that
night, she snuggled my neck and said, "It was the best birthday

ever, Daddy." I knew I couldn't compete with a mini circus, but I believed her nonetheless.

For the most part, we had had a great year with regular visits. Together, Natalie and I adhered to the schedule and it allowed us to share Meg equally. I hated admitting it, but Natalie had been accommodating and fair with the visitations. Meg and I even had a two-week vacation over Fourth of July. I was suspicious of Natalie's generosity as she usually didn't budge during holidays. Suspicions were confirmed, however, when Meg spilled the beans about her mommy taking a "vacation on a really big boat." At first, I had a twinge of feeling like she was taking advantage of me. But fourteen uninterrupted days with Meg was exciting, so I dropped it. Mom secured extra nursing staff for my grandmother allowing us to take Meg to a small cabin by the lake for a couple of days. Books, hikes, and a few sparklers were just the quiet quality time we all needed. Mom taught Meg to make chocolate chip cookies from scratch, and I taught her how to catch lightning bugs in a mason jar with the importance of setting them free again.

It was September, and Natalie had enrolled her in kindergarten, of which I wasn't particularly happy.

"Don't you think she's too young for school?" I questioned.

"No. *We* think she needs the socialization and jump start before first grade," she snapped.

We? Who's *we*? I didn't want to ask and give her the satisfaction of announcing a new man in her life. Natalie thought she was always the decision maker in our marriage. There was rarely a *we* decision. I'll be damned if some goofball steps in now and gets to be part of a *we* team. Even worse, she would tell me that the *nosy old bastard* was in on it, too. *Jump start? How big of a jump start would a five-year-old need before going to first grade?* Meg was a brilliantly talented little girl and light-years ahead of most snotty-nosed, messy-pants kids.

"I'll miss you this weekend, baby," I said. "But I'll see you next weekend, OK?"

"Yes, Daddy, and don't be sad!" she consoled.

The summer sped by like a bullet train, and I wasn't looking forward to the pending cold. I had just gotten used to working around the house in shorts and a T-shirt. I hated the thought of having to bundle up every time I needed to work on a gutter or window frame outside. The constant renovation of this house made the days fly into weeks, which turned into months. I felt as though repairs had become a never-ending story of pain, sweat, and money. Since the house was an inheritance, it was great to be worry free of a mortgage or rent. But the expenses were ripping through my savings faster than I could put it back in the bank. Several of the local merchants allowed me to hang fliers that offered my carpentry skills. I did the typical flier where you could rip off a phone number from the bottom tabs only to find it later shredded in your dryer. I got some calls, but they only led to a few running toilets and leaky gutters, none of which even paid for an occasional six-pack of cheap beer.

Drumming up business in a small town can be tough, especially at the tail end of a recession. People tend to get comfortable using the same old handyman for years, even if he does a shitty job. So there isn't much consideration or tolerance for the new guy in town. However, East Grayson's population was expanding, and the housing market was showing positive demand as a result. Although we were starting to pull out of the recession, growing families couldn't afford the city anymore and were looking to find bigger bang for their bucks in neighborhoods with nearby schools. Finally, I landed a job as head contractor for a building company. Their largest residential project was about to start in mid-September. It would slow down some of my own projects at the house, but I was willing to hire out a few of those chores in order to pull in a salary that could beef up my savings again. Truth was, I was looking forward to getting back into the world of real work. Even sharing the inappropriate guy camaraderie of beer and cursing with a few carpenters and painters after work sounded enticing. I wanted to celebrate my new job and decided to head to town.

As I walked through the square, ripping down my untouched fliers, I felt a sense of lightness and freedom. I was beginning to enjoy living alone again and not having to call home for every stop or move. The square was bustling with weekenders as there was a small tinge of fall in the air. It was still warm out, but businesses were decorating doorways with fake colorful leaves, bales of hay, and mini scarecrows. Small towns like East Grayson were havens for city dwellers trying to get away. Seasonal events and holidays brought in some badly needed cash for the merchants. With the influx of humanity, the crowded sidewalks felt more like home, and I was loving the feeling.

Last year, I had discovered a little deli in the town square that had wine tasting, and I was becoming a frequent visitor. It was cheap and had great food. Ted, the owner, hired me to rewire the place. He also commissioned me to make a new wooden sign for over the door. Ted was a no-frills kind of guy, born and raised in New Jersey. So the sign simply read *TED's*. He was nice and always overpaid me. He acted as though we had a secret club that belonged to us alone. I was welcome in his shop even after hours, and he had a way of showing great interest in my life while still respecting my privacy. Our friendship grew in a small amount of time, and I felt I had known him forever. He quickly became my respite from an albatross house. I wanted my light mood to last, so I stopped at Ted's café for a nice Malbec and whatever hearty pot he had simmering on the stove.

"Like lemmings to the sea, eh, Eli?" He smiled as I bounced in the door. Ted had a great sense of humor and always made me smile, despite myself. Although he was a lot older, we talked about many of the same subjects of likes and dislikes. We kept our conversations light and fun. I kept Ted's needs a priority in my schedule, and he showed his appreciation by sliding a big slab of fresh baked pie under my nose. Wine refills were usually free of charge as well.

"You don't have to feed me for life, you know." I grinned. "I got a job."

"I know, kid, but you've done so much for me!" he said. "A job? That's terrific! Wine's on me!" We both laughed. "Belly up. Tell me about the job! And how's the house coming along?"

"OK, I guess. The summer seems to have flown by, and I did get a lot done. Meg enjoyed her art station all summer. You should see the little books she creates. They're amazing!" I bragged. "And my mom helped with decorating the rest of her room. Looks nice!"

I rattled on and on, eventually describing my new job, a movie I had just seen, and so on. I talked more to Ted than anyone else in town. I missed my dad and some of my New York friends. Ted helped fill that void. But, quite frankly, I was tired of talking about the house. I was beginning to think it was all I *could* talk about. Unlike him, I hadn't read a good book in so long that I was suspicious I had forgotten how to read. I missed reading. It had been my favorite alone time when at NYU. I loved those times at Washington Square Park in between classes, reading alone and feeling invisible. It created a sanctuary that I craved every day. Natalie would consistently remind me how I had wasted my time in college.

"You'll never find a job with a degree in history!" she'd say with a smirk.

My final decision to choose a career in carpentry gave her just the ammunition to belittle my college career.

"I just don't understand you, Eli," she mumbled frequently.

The feeling was mutual. Maybe she was right. I had signed up for all the classes that truly interested me without any intention of ever using them to further a career. I was a carpenter by choice, but I wanted to satisfy my parent's desire to help provide me with an education. They accepted my passion but insisted that I wouldn't regret the education. In the long run, they were right. Although I didn't use the degree for a specific career, getting a college degree allowed me to accept jobs in my career of choice with bigger *white-collar* titles and better salaries—better than the undereducated men on the job who were referred to as *blue collar*, and yet just talented. As well, I was able to enjoy friends with common interest who were well read and could talk about an array of subjects.

But I couldn't help but think about her choices as well. Natalie went to a private liberal arts college. The *nosey old bastard* picked up the tab. She spent four years taking core classes in English literature. Then, two months after graduating, she signed up for an online course in interior design. Her days were spent advising upper-class friends and family on the importance of texture, color, and proper staging of the home. Designer pillows were her specialty. The kind with little beads and sparkly shit glued to the front. You couldn't rest your head on one. If the beads and sparkly shit didn't slice up your face, your wife would when she caught you using it under your sweaty head. They were for *show only*, and I simply saw them as a symbol of her pretentious attitude.

It wasn't until Ted asked me about the house that I remembered Bertha's newspaper. The single page had become a fixed dusty object on the hall table and hadn't been touched since its discovery. I was still interested, but I put had it on the back burner over the summer to either focus on the house or my visits with Meg.

I settled at the counter ready to embrace an escape of good food and Ted.

"Have you met any of your neighbors?" he asked.

"Well, a few. I went to the Friends of East Grayson meeting almost a year ago. It was pretty much old people and women." I shrugged. He let out a great belly laugh. I purposely left out the fact that I had slam-dunked a young woman when trying to ditch early. I wasn't sure I wanted talk about women with anyone, yet. I didn't want to give the impression I was ready to start dating or was even looking. And any inquiries about that felt too invasive at this point.

A few months before, Ted and I had sat out back on his loading dock with wine and cigars after closing the shop. We talked about my divorce, but I kept it brief with most of the details under lock. Of the few scenarios I did mention, Ted just offered an all-knowing nod. To deflect the conversation from me, I asked him if he had ever been married.

"Divorced once, widowed once," he offered.

"Wow. Want to elaborate on that?" I encouraged.

"I got married right after graduating from high school, Brooklyn, class of '52." He settled back in his chair. "She was pregnant, a prom night that wasn't thought out carefully, so to speak. We were just kids, and it was a real mess. Eventually, so was the marriage. We divorced about two years after my son was born. Unfortunately, she moved West and took Jake with her. She and her family were like a group of gypsies. Never staying in one place for very long. Eventually, I lost track of them. I never saw him again. You know, the days before technology. Hell, now you can track anybody!" he laughed.

He paused for a while and waited for a loud motorcycle to pass.

"Eventually, I met my second wife, Cynthia. I was thirty-one and divorced. Certainly, older, wiser, and making a little more money than the first time. I was a bartender in Brooklyn. She was a twenty-eight-year-old aspiring actress, seeking Broadway. She came into the bar looking for part-time work. Prettiest thing you have ever seen. Great smile, great figure, and funny. She always made me laugh. I fell in love immediately. I convinced the owner to hire her. And eventually, she convinced me to marry her." He laughed and slapped me on the back. "It didn't take much! I was married to that wonderful woman for thirty-two years. She never made it to Broadway but stayed active in small theater groups, eventually getting into costuming. She could make any costume you needed! When we got older, she encouraged me to move here and open up shop ten years ago, you know, get outta Brooklyn." He hesitated, took a puff, and sighed, "She got breast cancer and died five years after we moved. Cynthia was the love of my life."

"I'm sorry," I said. "Did you have any children by her?"

"Nope."

Silence blanketed the moment. Eventually, Ted looked over at me and smiled. He had the most content expression I had ever seen on another human being, and I was jealous. The man had just shared the most horrendous loss of love, and I couldn't help but wonder if I would ever feel that kind of love, if I would ever know contentment in a relationship. Like crossing streams at a campfire, we had shared a male-bonding moment that night of understood commonality. Content, we silently puffed our stogies and stared out at the empty parking lot. We hadn't discussed Jake or Cynthia since.

The storefront door swung open, and I glanced up. The glare of sun bouncing off the glass briefly blinding me, and all I could see was a silhouette. "Penny!" he called out. It was her! It was *the* smile! I had seen her around town from time to time. We waved across different check out aisles at the grocery store. Once, I was pulling into the Oil Change Express just as she was pulling out. I waved but she didn't see me. We actually had a brief conversation one morning when I walked out to my mailbox and she was leaving for school. Her actions were hurried, so the conversation was quick and unmemorable—except the last statement as she drove off and shouted out her window, "Let's get together soon!" But then summer came, and somehow, even though I meandered on my front porch getting the newspaper, checking my mail, pretending to check out the flora and fauna in my yard, I never saw her. Not all summer.

So here she was, smiling and greeting everyone in the café, being her typical joyful self. Trying not to appear too anxious and excited, I put my soup directly under my chin where I could stick the spoon in my mouth at every opportunity. I stirred, blew, sipped, and stirred some more while Ted and Penny chatted. I was proud of my nonchalant act—downright award winning. And then she turned to me.

"Hi!" Penny appeared to glow. "Great to see you again, Eli!" She gently patted my arm.

"Yes," I managed to mutter as I quickly grabbed up my napkin to catch any potential soup drool. "You too!"

"Oh! You two know each other?" Ted inquired.

"Yes!" Penny smiled. "We met at the FEG meeting. Or I should say *bumped* into one another!" she elbowed me and snorted a goofy laugh as though we were long-lost friends. "Gosh, that was almost a year ago! Why haven't I seen you? And we're neighbors, for gosh sakes!"

"Neighbors!" Ted cocked his head in my direction. With a roguish grin, he wiggled his eyebrows up and down like Groucho. "How convenient!"

A small stream of sweat trickled down my back inside my shirt, sending an uncomfortable chill up my spine. I slightly smiled and ducked my face back into the soup bowl.

Penny continued, "How's it going, Eli?"

"Good! Good!" I nodded. "How about you? Been out of town?" I bravely asked her. "I haven't seen you out and about in quite a while."

"Yep. As soon as school got out, I headed to the beach for the summer. I mooched off family, and it was great!" She pushed up her shirt sleeve and tapped her bronzed forearm. "Check it out: got a little sun! How was your summer? Go anywhere?"

"Eli is renovating his house!" Ted interjected before I could answer. "I can't wait to see it!" He slapped me on the back and walked away. I couldn't help but grin, secretly grateful for all the prompting.

"Oh, Eli!" she said. "It's a great house with so much potential. I hope you'll invite us to a housewarming."

As she spoke she floated past me with one hand on my arm and gently squeezed, all in one sweeping motion. Her mannerisms were comforting. She was close without stifling and appeared to move as if skating on ice.

"Must run, everyone! Saw you all through the window and had to say hello!" she called out as she headed to the door.

"Aren't you going to stay and have a glass of wine with us?" Ted pouted.

"Can't today, but I'll definitely be in Friday after school this week!" she promised. "You know what they say: Veni, vidi, vino!"

She was out the door as quickly as she had come in, tucking her blond hair carelessly under a baseball cap. I kept staring out through the glass door as if she might come back announcing she had forgotten something or possibly changed her mind about that vino. I quietly wished she would. She had a wonderful carefree way about her. But she disappeared around the corner.

"Veni, vidi, vino?" A man at the end of the counter smirked. "What the hell does that mean?"

"I came. I saw. I conquered," I muttered.

"Close!" Ted laughed.

4

It is not the length of life, but the depth.
—Ralph Waldo Emerson

I PUT BUCKETS ON the floor to accommodate constant drips from the ceiling in most rooms. The deafening ping was a reminder that the outside of the house needed just as much attention as the inside. In my attempt to make order out of chaos for Meg, I ignored that the roof was probably just as old as the house. Clearly, it needed to be addressed, but to find a dry spell was going to be difficult. The fall brought a lot of rain to the northeast. But this time it appeared to be backed up by some far away hurricane. It was a torrential downpour, for sure. Oddly, I found it somewhat calming and preferred to sit at my kitchen table. With coffee in hand, I just stared out the window.

I used the weather as an excuse to avoid chores on a rainy weekend. All work on the new job was basically on hold as well. I had spent the past week running around and ensuring my crew on the jobsite had all tools, bare lumber, and so on covered and secured until we could get back to construction. Enjoying the rainy Saturday was the catalyst to my inner peace and contentment, and I was savoring the moment. It was probably just exhaustion, and I couldn't feel anything. The constant streams and unpredictable paths of water running down the large window were mesmerizing. I understood why this was Meg's favorite place to sit in the morning. She was content to observe the outside world and quietly soak in all the peace it offered.

Observing Meg was just the mentorship I needed. My five-year-old was teaching me, a grown man, how to start my day. I was envious of her ability to see only the beauty and secretly wished I could keep her isolated from change forever. I wanted to hold on to her and allow her to create nothing but good. I missed Meg every day she wasn't here, and the more I thought about it, the more my inner peace started to fade. I was painfully aware that my own thoughts were my worst enemies. Friends and family marveled at my energy level. "Where do you get it all, Eli?" they frequently asked. They failed to understand that I had to keep moving, keep busy physically to settle my brain. For me, too much thought brought too much anxiety.

As I turned from the window, I scanned the room, looking for any imperfection that would inspire me back into work. Certainly, there were many, so I would have to focus, focus on one job that would push me from emotional to physical.

Just as I fixated on the ugly rusted hardware of the metal cabinets, my doorbell rang. I smirked considering how my mother would say that "angels were intervening." I considered ignoring it. But the downpour of the rain raised my curiosity, and I couldn't imagine anyone coming out in such hideous weather unless it was important.

It rang several times before I could respond. I was grateful *something* was working in the house. I put down my cup and made my way to the front door. Condensation on the glass distorted the view to the outside, and all I could decipher was a shadowy figure. I squinted and bobbed my head back and forth trying to see but finally gave up and jerked open the door. It was Penny. She wore a yellow slick raincoat and rubber boots. As she peered from under the hood and all that yellow vinyl, there was no mistaking that smile.

"Sorry!" I yelled above the downpour. "Come on in! I didn't recognize you at first."

"Hi!" She laughed as she entered the doorway.

Frantically she tried to wipe her feet on a wooden floor void of a proper welcome mat.

"Oh, gosh! I'm dripping water all over your floor!" She frowned.

I simply pointed to the three collection buckets nearby, and we both laughed.

"I'm really sorry to bother you, and I won't stay, I promise," she continued. "I made some banana nut bread and thought you could use a little yummy on such a crappy day."

She stretched out her arms and handed me a neatly wrapped loaf in aluminum foil. I immediately raised the warm bundle to my nose and savored it for a moment. Since I had been living off frozen dinners and the occasional Chinese takeout and pizza delivery, anything fresh from the oven was a terrific gift.

"Thank you," I said. "Would you like some coffee?"

Please stay.

"Are you sure?" she asked. "I mean, I don't want to bother you on a day off."

"Please." I stretched out my free hand and motioned for her coat.

She flipped down the hood and kicked off her boots. Slowly, she walked a few steps in a large circle gazing all around up and down as she slipped out of her raincoat.

"This is amazing!" she squealed. "I can't believe what you've done already!"

I loved the compliment but was almost leery of its earnestness. I still had a lot of tools laying around in the parlor like uninvited guests that would never leave. Certainly, the buckets of water that were scattered about couldn't be mistaken for anything less than a work still in progress. And I only took the time to sweep up sawdust when I knew Meg was coming.

"Well, I certainly have a lot more work to do on this old place," I shyly apologized.

"No, really, it is wonderful!" she went on. "Bertie was so tidy and particular about all of her little things placed ever so neatly. But if you don't mind me saying, this house was a little old lady's house." She chuckled. "So far, you have managed to update and still keep the integrity of its age. It looks great and I can't wait to see what you will do next!" She patted me on the arm. I was beginning to see she did that often—and I liked it.

I was so flattered that I was embarrassed and really wasn't sure what to say next. I wanted to offer a tour of the rest of the house, but I couldn't remember the state of my bedroom or bathroom and was horrified at the possible discoveries we would find together.

So I kept the tour on the main level and guided her through the house into the kitchen. After more kudos for my handiwork, Penny and I finally settled at the kitchen table with coffee and banana bread. We chatted for hours about the town, recent movies, and a few of the books we had both enjoyed. She asked me all about my favorite subject, Meg, and appeared interested and delighted at every detail. After a couple of hours, I realized that time had slipped into the early afternoon. I would have been content to sit there into the evening. Gone was the anxiety of work and projects. Her smile and baked goods were just the warm spot I craved and what kept the cold dreary rain outside.

"I should really leave you alone!" she exclaimed. "I certainly didn't mean to overstay my welcome."

"Glad you came." I smiled. "Thanks again for the banana bread."

"You are very welcome and thank for sharing it!" She laughed. "I'll make you more!"

I followed her down the hallway toward the front door. I took the opportunity to quickly scan her with my eyes. She had a certain comfortable style about her. Penny's hair was a mass of soft golden curls. She had managed to harness it into a twisted bright yellow handkerchief creating a thick knot on the top of her head. Her T-shirt, jeans, and bare feet were an obvious display of comfort and confidence. She had been baking at home and saw no pretentious reason to change such comfort when visiting a neighbor, a friend. I grinned with approval. She was a sunny breath of fresh air on a rainy miserable fall day. I quickly grabbed her raincoat and held it out. I hadn't had sex since well before my divorce, and I must admit, a shapely woman's body could send the white surrender flag up the pole. No pun intended.

Toward the end of my marriage, I found myself falling asleep on the couch more and more. The only glow on my face was from the TV in the dark room. I taught myself to flip the designer pillows over, beads face down to protect my face, and rubbed my sweaty head into the feathered nook. In the morning, I flipped it back and placed it neatly in a corner of the couch. The stains of my sweat were my revenge and remained hidden as Natalie no longer joined me there. There used to be an occasional fuck on that couch, usually after too much wine. Eventually, the couch became nothing but a staged presence in an empty, awkward room. I had convinced myself that celibacy was now the norm for me, void an occasional liaison with myself. Lately, I was even too tired for that.

On the way out, Penny paused at the old table in the front hall. It was one of Bertha's favorite pieces, made by my grandfather and dad together. The worn and scratched surfaces were in need of restoration. Until I could tackle that job, I liked the convenience of throwing my keys and mail on something other than the floor when I walked through the door. Penny's fingers slowly and gently stroked the carved details.

"I loved Bertie and miss her," she stated softly.

I was ashamed as I hadn't thought about my great-aunt Bertha once, as a person, for a long time. For me, her very being was transposed through old furniture and cat hair. I had convinced myself that the old musty smell of the house had come from her and was just another oddity about her that made me feel uncomfortable all those years.

"We had some lovely afternoon chats with tea, and I found her life stories and wisdom so fascinating and comforting," she volunteered.

She was talking about the little old Jewish woman with all the cats, the one who periodically blurted out something in Yiddish and then threw her head back in a big toothy laugh, like we all got the joke. *Bless her heart!*

I decided to excuse myself. "I really didn't know her. I mean, we visited her often and saw each other every weekend when I was growing up. But we didn't talk much." I continued, "She would pinch my cheeks and squeeze me until I couldn't breathe anymore. Then I just ran outside and kicked a soccer ball around until time to leave. Right after graduating from high school, I moved to New York."

"Oh, she was an amazing woman!" she insisted. "You were just a kid, and I can see why you didn't really hang out in here." She laughed.

Suddenly, Penny's hand stopped at the newspaper that I had tossed down and forgotten.

"What's this?" she inquired. "Oh, I'm sorry! Nosey, huh?!"

"No, that's ok," I reassured her. "I found it when gutting a closet upstairs in Meg's room. I've been wanting to research it but just haven't had the time."

"Oh, wow!" she exclaimed excitedly. "I *love* this kind of stuff! Mind if I take a closer look?"

"Go ahead," I said. "I noticed Bertha's name on one of the articles. I'm a little surprised. I never knew she wrote for a German newspaper. But I don't understand the German, so I have no clue what it's about."

I reached across and pointed to Bertha's name. After several minutes, Penny excitedly placed her hand on the page and quickly looked up at me.

"Oh, Eli," she gasped. "Bertie used to tell me stories about working at this paper."

"I'm a little shocked by it," I continued. "I mean…maybe it isn't really *journalism*. Maybe it's just an article about cooking or manners or something."

"I don't know what she was writing about here, Eli," Penny said, shaking her head. "Although she told me little stories here and there, she kept much of it light and brief. She rarely discussed what was going on with the pending war or even being Jewish. Most of the time, she would give me little stories about a friendship, her apartment with the garden…you know, things like that."

She continued, "If I questioned too much, she would just gear the conversation into another direction, like cooking, her cats, the weather. I didn't want to press her with a lot of questions. She was a very private person, and I wanted to respect that. But I will tell you this, Eli." She leaned in like she was sharing a secret. "I always had the feeling there was a lot more to Bertha's story. I could tell when she would just cut our conversation short."

"I wonder what the article is about," I said as my interest started to pique.

My grandmother, Freida, probably could still translate it, but I didn't really want to ask. Since moving into assisted living, visits were kept short and sweet. Grandma was never told of any family drama and Mom had become overly protective of her.

Penny offered to take the paper and get it translated by the German language teacher at the high school. I slid the newspaper into a large freezer bag to protect it from the rain. She slipped it under her slicker and hollered as she ran out the door.

"I'll take good care of it, Eli, I promise!"

I watched as she trotted down the steps and ran across the street. I felt content and unconcerned for the paper's safe keeping. Besides, it was another excuse to see her again. Although I hadn't known Penny long, I trusted her. And trusting others wasn't something I did very well. But I could feel she was different. And the feeling was good.

5

Sometimes our light goes out,
but is blown again into instant flame by an
encounter with another human being.
—Albert Schweitzer

"HEY! I JUST found out some info about Bertie's newspaper article. Give me a call. Let's have vino later. My place this time…oh, this is Penny."

Penny and I had exchanged cell numbers on that rainy afternoon, but I didn't have the nerve to be the first to call. It had only been a week, and I didn't want to look needy. I had forgotten she had the newspaper. Quite honestly, I was more interested in her than an old, dusty paper. I was excited by her call, and like a schoolkid, I listened to it several times. I didn't need to save it, but I did anyway. I convinced myself it was important, and I may need to refer to it at some point later in the day.

Yeah, right. I couldn't even fool myself and laughed. I didn't call back immediately. I had to think about how I would bow out. It was my weekend to have Meg, and I hadn't seen her for the past two weekends. Although Penny's invitation gave my attitude a new jump start, Meg's visits were precious to me and canceling with her was never an option. Secretly, I felt relieved. As much as I wanted to see

Penny again, doing so created anxiety. Since my divorce, I avoided dating like the plague. I had developed excuses that formed a brick wall of fake confidence and appeared comfortable with that decision. Friends and family persisted with encouraging clichés and quips: "When the right one comes along," "when you least expect it," "your soulmate," and my all-time favorite "get back in the saddle again." The whole thing was ridiculous.

"No thanks!" I shouted, throwing my hands in the air. "I'm wearing Eau d'Repel a Girl, and it's working quite nicely."

Sarcasm was my friend, and that line always got a laugh and endeared me as the self-assured, content bachelor. It was a sure way to put a screeching halt to the conversation. There were times it was so convincing that I had fallen for it myself, positive that they were all envious of me. I was never going *there* again, and I decided that my best bet was to stay focused. Focus on Meg, the house, and just pushing through it all. Keeping my body busy was the best way to keep my mind sane.

I had purchased a bike when I moved to Grayson. Some guys choose the big Harley for their midlife journeys. I valued my life and chose the kind with pedals. Originally, it was to get exercise. But the more I rode the better I felt emotionally, too. Peddling at a constant pace created a sense of distance—distance that created space—space that allowed peace. And it was that same peddling that helped me focus. So it was decided. I threw on my clothes and ran down the stairs and into the garage. There weren't too many more weeks before the weather would get too cold for cycling. I was headed out on my mission.

I was pumping hard, probably harder than usual. But within a short period of time I started to feel the weight melt off me. It wasn't physical weight. Although I certainly could have used some attention around my gut, that area where men first start showing their age and compensate by boasting about the love handles. *Love handles, my ass!* Ironically, there was no *love* about it. My excess blubber was a direct result of beer, wine, and absence of sex. I drank more and more those last few married years seeking the self-induced coma I so desperately needed. I thought if I knocked back a few, just enough to take the edge off that bad attitude I was so frequently accused of, I would feel better about how sad and trapped I felt. And possibly—just possibly—I could turn it all around. Make it better. Make it work. The reality was I just wanted to make it go away. Well, it did. And it was all replaced with baggage and blubber.

I pedaled harder. I pedaled harder to get rid of the blubber. I pedaled harder to get rid of the baggage. The mental baggage that kept me up at night. The baggage that appeared to get heavier and heavier and no matter how hard I tried that baggage was locked tight. I carried it around, all the low self-esteem and anger I could possibly pack and then slapped down the padlocks, threw away the key, and paraded my baggage like a great martyr. I really wasn't kidding myself, and I doubt anyone else. But the peddling helped, and I needed it. If nothing else, after about five miles, I was too exhausted to give a shit anymore.

I rounded the corner back down my street and was headed home. Penny stood happily on the sidewalk directly in front of my garage. She was smiling and beautiful. *Damn it!* I was unprepared. I didn't know what I was going to say. I hadn't practiced my response. It was important to me to not sound stupid, uninterested, and yet, not go in the direction of needy. I slowed to a stop with a convenient five to six feet distance. Of course, that didn't stop her. She beamed and bounced right up to me.

"I couldn't wait for you to get home!" She did a small jump up and down like a little kid. Her appearance and demeanor were typical Penny. Her face was scrubbed clean of makeup. Some of her wild, curly hair was pulled up into a ponytail that was carelessly skewed to the side of her head. She'd missed some of it, and it softly framed her bare face. She had on baggy pants that looked like pajama bottoms, a white tank top with no bra, and flip-flops. I hadn't been this turned on in years.

"How was your ride? We should ride together sometime. Are you free tonight? We can call out for Chinese and a little wine." She smiled.

Her rapid fire caught me off guard, and I began to stammer. I could feel the words exit my mouth but felt very little control.

"I promised her pizza. She loves pizza. I need to pick her up at three," was all I could muster.

"Little Meg? Bring her, and we can do pizza." She placed her hand on my sweaty arm. "We can play scrabble or something. I would love to have you both. And my friend, the German teacher I told you about, translated Bertie's article! I'm dying to show you! Come on. Just do it!" she encouraged with a gentle punch to my arm.

I felt myself float as if in a pool of water. All stress was melting at a rapid speed, and a sense of calm engulfed me. Maybe it was just from pedaling hard on my ride. But I had experienced this same feeling before. It was on that rainy afternoon with her at my kitchen table. She had an incredible way of making everything seem easy and simple.

"If you're sure. I mean...," I shrugged.

She stopped me before I blundered further. "Yes, of course. It'll be fun. See you at five thirtyish!" she shouted over her shoulder as she jogged back home.

There it was. My evening was basically planned out with little effort or stress. I looked forward to picking up Meg and a relaxing evening with Penny. She was quickly becoming a good friend and I treasured that. *I better wear my Eau d'Repel a Girl. Focus. And suck in your gut!*

The evening had gone perfect. Meg appeared to love Penny, and Penny played and talked to Meg as if they had been friends forever. It was relaxing and the most fun I could remember. Penny's attention to details made us both feel welcomed and at home. Pizza, fresh baked cinnamon cookies, and sitting on the floor around the coffee table in front of a fire while everybody kicked off their shoes was perfect. It was just the right atmosphere for calm conversation. Meg was always included, and she giggled constantly. After a round of Eye Spy with My Little Eye, Meg curled up on my lap and quietly fell asleep in my arms. Penny leaned over and peaked at Meg.

"Shhhhhh. Stay right there," she whispered as she slowly got up and went into the kitchen. When she returned, she was carrying two glasses of red wine and a small blanket.

"This was my binky when I was a little girl," she said quietly and carefully placed it across Meg's lap.

While still on the floor, we silently sipped wine. Never had I felt this comfortable in silence with a woman. Silence with Natalie meant somebody was pissed off and void of communication. Silence with Penny was a chance to breathe.

"I wanted to tell you about the article Bertie wrote in the *Die Rote Fahne*. Most definitely, it was not about recipes, manners, or anything like that, Eli." She rolled her eyes.

She reached behind me and grabbed the article off a side table. Together, we scanned the translation in the glow of the fireplace. It was clearly a movie review, and Bertha was giving a synopsis of its release in Berlin. I had seen this movie in college when I'd taken a film history class for fun. *Metropolis* was one of the films we studied. It was awesome and frightening at the same time. Evidently, Bertha was just a film critic. Or was she? It was 1927 in Germany, and *Metropolis* was all about a master plan at separating classes. It was criticized for its communist overtones. I had a film history professor who was an old hippy, and he loved it.

After reading the translation, I leaned forward and placed the paper on the coffee table, freeing my arms to wrap up Meg in the borrowed blanket. The article was fascinating, and I was grateful to Penny. But I wanted to soak up the lovely moment. When I leaned back, her face was directly in front of mine. In the glow of the fire, her skin and hair appeared golden and warm. She smelled of cinnamon cookies.

She whispered, "Well, what do you think?"

I tilted my head, leaned in slowly, and softly, I kissed her.

6

The two most important days in your life
are the day you were born
and the day you find out why.
—Mark Twain

I WOKE UP WITH more energy than I can remember, and my thoughts immediately had gone to last night. A quick scan of the room drew my attention to the old alarm clock on the side table. I questioned the validity of the screen: 5:45 a.m. I was wide awake, and the room was still dark. I couldn't remember the last time I had been up before dawn. I had a list of things I wanted to accomplish this morning and they weren't house related.

My anxiety about last night started to kick in. I couldn't believe I had kissed her. Questioning whether it was the right thing to do or not so early in the friendship started the usual anxiety. Certainly, Penny's reaction shouldn't give me any reason for concern. After I kissed her, she shyly looked down and smiled. For a brief moment, she nuzzled her face into my neck and rested her head on my shoulder. Together, we silently stared into the fire when our hypnotic trance was broken by Meg's sudden jerk. Half asleep, she started to squirm and whine. Penny smiled, patted Meg on her back, and got up to take the wine glasses to the kitchen.

"I should get her home," I whispered.

"Of course, let me help you," Penny replied as she put the glasses back down and reached for Meg.

Together, we hung onto Meg as I struggled to stand after sitting on the floor so long. We stifled our laughter at the clumsy scenario of two adults attempting to manipulate a wiggling child. In her sleepy stupor, Meg was trying to get comfortable in my arms. Clearly, her legs were getting too long to be held, and we both wobbled across the room.

Meg was the perfect barrier between two people caught in that awkward goodbye-at-the-door moment. To kiss again or not to kiss again, that was the question. I thanked Penny, handed her the small blanket, and started to make my way out to the porch. She stopped me and placed the blanket back over Meg, snuggly securing it around her shoulders.

"I'll get it later." She patted us both. My exit felt swift, controlled, and consensual.

While getting Meg into her pajamas and tucked into bed, I smiled, thinking about how much I had enjoyed the evening with Penny. Once covered and comfortable, Meg turned over and quickly dozed off again. For a moment, I sat on the edge, stroked her hair, and listened to her soft, rhythmic breaths. I felt really happy. All my hard labor on the house was coming to fruition, and we were starting to reap the benefits. I had concentrated on the heating system, ductwork, and insulation throughout the summer, making the house a lot less drafty and a hell of a lot warmer for the pending winter. Meg loved her new room and I loved seeing her in it.

It was still early, so I made my way down the stairs to clean up the neglected dishes from earlier in the day. As I started to turn the corner toward the kitchen, there was a light tap on the door. Puzzled, I peeked out to see Penny on my porch. She smiled, waved, and held up the envelope to clarify her presence. I quickly opened the door.

"I thought you might like to look at this again in the morning with your coffee," she said. She stretched out her arm from the porch and handed me the envelope.

"Oh, thanks. You didn't need to do that," I said. "I could have gotten it later." I secretly wished she hadn't. It would have given me an excuse to *drop in* on her the next day. But then again, I still had her childhood blanket.

"No worries, see you later." She leaned forward, placed one foot across the threshold while keeping one foot out. She grabbed my arm and kissed me on the cheek. "Good night." She smiled as she turned and jogged back across the street. Later, I had a hard time going to sleep, replaying it all in my head. But once I dozed off, I slept like a rock. Rising before dawn was starting to grab hold of me, and I scurried out of bed like a little kid.

Penny's information about the newspaper clipping had startled me. Never in my wildest imagination could I have placed Bertha there. What she had written was astounding. Although brief, it was well written and interesting. But it was frightening as well. Maybe I was just letting my imagination get the best of me. After all, it was just a movie review. *But wasn't she afraid? Didn't she know what was coming? Was she planning her escape, or did she have the chutzpah to stick it out and fight?*

My knowledge of the Holocaust was limited to a whitewashed school curriculum. And, although I am Jewish, I am far from Orthodox. I knew staggering statics of the atrocities. To succumb to the depressing annual remembrances was something I just couldn't do. I knew my history and it was in the past, where it belonged. My grandparents had lived in England for a few years before coming to America in their midtwenties. Hence, my parents were born here in the States, and that is exactly what I always thought of them as—Americans. Nothing more.

And as for Bertha, I knew she had lived in London before coming here as well. But I never really knew for how long and exactly when she'd arrived. Nor had I asked. There were no numbered tattoos on any of their arms; they appeared happy and healthy. So I assumed they were fine. They had gotten out unscathed. And I was just a kid—busy with soccer, school, and just plain surviving the torment from bullying classmates. My own past was painful enough. Why invite more?

I threw on my clothes and hurried down the stairs. I needed to get her back to her mother before lunch. Natalie's rules. For a few weeks, she wanted Meg to be home a day early to ensure they had all day Sunday to get ready for Monday morning school. A little over the top in my opinion, but my opinion didn't matter. I had a few hours to gather my thoughts and make some plans for the day. As I made my way to the kitchen where I could be close to the coffee, I grabbed the news article off the hall table and the print-out translation Penny had given me the night before. I was excited and curious to sit and study it for myself.

My newfound interest in Bertha was surging, and I had become intrigued as to when and how she got to this house. If I was going to live here, I wanted to know what brought her here, too. Perhaps this house was just as much an escape for her as it has been for me. Maybe Bertha ran away from the Nazis just as I ran away from interactions with other kids and adults and a debilitating marriage. There certainly wasn't a comparison between her escape from a brutal murdering and oppressive regime to my insecurities and fear of bullies and a bitchy wife, although Natalie would have made a great SS. Perhaps finding out more about Bertha's survival would help me put my past into a perspective of lighter note.

With coffee in hand, I sat at the kitchen table and placed the article and its translation in front of me. My eyes scanned back and forth between the original in German and the English supplement. I had quickly read it last night and remembered briefly some of the details. However, last night I had been distracted. When Penny returned from her kitchen with wine, she'd slid in behind the coffee table onto the floor next to me so that she could read along over my shoulder. She helped hold the other side of the paper, freeing my other arm for my sleeping daughter. Her shoulder pressed against mine, the scent of her hair, the candlelight, the wine, and knowing Meg was safe in my arms was a moment of contentment and peace. Reading and concentrating, however, was difficult. And finally, quite honestly, the spontaneity of our impulsive kiss rushed all the blood from my brain, and I remember very little of the article's details.

The Die Rote Fahne:

The Die Rote Fahne was a periodical based in Berlin. It ran from 1918 to 1933. Many prominent Germans worked on the paper. Translated, it was called The Red Flag. It was briefly banned from 1923–1924 for its ties to the Communist Party. In 1933, the Nazi police closed the doors at the Karl-Liebknecht-Haus. An underground continued printing and distributing the paper well into the 1940s, sometimes under the name Rote Sturmafahne *(Red Storm Flag) or* Die Fahne der Revolution *(The Flag of the Revolution).*

Once again, Metropolis *has graced our theaters. This new opening is a shorter version of the previously shown film in January at the Ufa-Palast am Zoo. Although well received to record crowds with standing ovations and critics' praise, approximately 118 minutes has been cut from the original. Alfred Hugenberg recently took charge of Ufa and immediately halted distribution of the film until contents relating to "communism and religious imagery" were eradicated during editing.*

Thankfully, the beautifully executed film tolerated the brief intrusion and appeared to have little impact on its further public embrace. Thankfully, Metropolis *will continue to be enjoyed and embraced as a monumental and poignant achievement for years to come.*

1927
Metropolis Again!
By Bertha Plesser

And there it was. She was bat-shit crazy and possibly a communist. That didn't really bother me too much. But it was pulling me deeper into her story, for sure.

I was startled by the loud roar and crashing of the garbage trucks. Time was flying by, and I needed to get Meg up, dressed, and fed. My research would have to wait until the afternoon. My roof would have to wait for another day. *Hell, I have plenty of buckets!*

Dropping Meg off at the usual meeting spot was always difficult. But the strip mall on a Saturday was even worse. The parking lot was loud and crowded with weekend shoppers. Adding in the mix of chaotic parents with their brood of unruly kids trying to get last minute back-to-school sales made it unbearable. I missed Meg before Natalie's car was even out of sight. The polite exchange between Natalie and me was forced and uncomfortable, and I resented her for that. So I pulled off the bandage and with a fast-tight hug and an *I love you, baby*, I reluctantly handed her over.

With a swift and deliberate grab, Natalie took Meg by the hand and began conversation with her as if I wasn't there. I could hear Meg holler over her shoulder, "I love you, too, Da—" as Natalie whisked her into the car and slammed the door. I'd see Meg again within the next few weeks. But the pain of watching her ride off, knowing that she wasn't truly all mine all the time, made it feel as though she was just on loan to me—on loan for brief moments without real control of when and how I would see her again. I had to stay strong and healthy for her and wait for our next weekend together. But the pain of the goodbye always stuck with me and made my future feel uneasy and uncertain.

The only way to move past the feeling of gloom was to focus, focus on whatever project I was dedicated to at the time. This time, it wasn't the house. Although I was far from done with the needed projects that were plentiful, I was focused on finding out the true story about Bertha. I continued to question my motives. I did wonder why I was so suddenly interested. But there was a gut feeling that it was something I needed to know. The curiosity had quickly become obsession.

I spent the rest of the afternoon at the local East Grayson Public Library. I hadn't been in a library in years and was surprised at how much I enjoyed it. The quiet surroundings, browsing through the books and periodicals—I loved the peace and quiet. My time was uninterrupted and productive. The librarian was a sweet, middle-aged woman eager to help. She was intrigued with my quest and attempted to provide me with everything I needed via microfiche and periodicals. I saved any internet search for later when I could use my own laptop and wine. It didn't take long before I had the exact information I needed. The *Die Rote Fahne* had been one of Germany's most liberal newspapers and among thousands that were taken over by the Nazis. In October of 1933, all Jewish editors and journalists, as well as anyone deemed too liberal or communist, were ousted from their positions. Jewish owners were pressured to sell their newspapers at below market prices, forcing them into bankruptcy. Eventually, Hitler controlled the newspapers, radio, and newsreels. As Nazi propaganda fueled the potential possibilities of communism spreading throughout the press, anxiety and fear allowed the German people to become vulnerable to Hitler's ultimate control and occupation.

I was fascinated by the timeline of the German press. I was so intent on what I was reading that I realized I had lost all track of time.

I still had no information as to when Bertha left the newspaper. This was extremely alarming as my research provided the facts that the founders of the newspaper, Rosa Luxemburg and Karl Liebknecht, were arrested, interrogated, and executed by a firing squad January 15, 1919. By my math calculations, Bertha would have only been about fourteen years old during that time. But the history of that paper, and the dangers that already existed before Bertha's arrival should have alerted her and sent her running long before. Yet she still took the job.

And equally important to me was where she went from there. It became painfully clear that I was going to have to ask Mom for any information she might have about Bertha. I wasn't hopeful at this point. Mom never talked about Bertha's past. If she had known anything exciting, intriguing, and especially scandalous, my mother would have been the town crier. She wouldn't have been able to contain herself. She loved a good story.

Meanwhile, happy hour was approaching, and I felt the need to hit Ted's café. A glass of wine, some of his best shepherd's pie, not to mention a little camaraderie, was just how I wanted to end the day. I had no plans to discuss any of this with him. I had learned along the way that revealing my projects, plans, or any part of my life only opened the forum for too many questions and way too much advise on how to proceed. I already had it planned. Ted had once knighted me as "the king of suspense," and he was probably right. My projects and activities were mine. I was now in possession of them in spirit and time and saw no reason to share them. Besides, at this point, I wasn't sure there was much to share.

I left Mom a voice mail asking her over for coffee and scones in the morning. Although my hesitation persisted, I did look forward to our time together, uninterrupted and relaxed. I loved my mom and have had some amazing laughs and good times with her. Truth be told, I have felt closer to her than anyone else since Dad passed away, and especially since my divorce. Together, we have shared our bond of love and attention for Meg, and my little girl was the human glue. Mom had always said to me, "There's no understanding the love I feel for you, Eli, until you have a child of your own. Then you will know." She was right.

"Eli!" Ted cheered. "Belly up to the bar, kid!"

Ahhhh, veni, vidi, vino.

7

Life's under no obligation to give us what we expect.
—Margaret Mitchell

"YOUR VOICE MAIL indicated that you found something interesting in the house and wanted me to see it?" Mom asked. "That's exciting! I'll be there!"

I ran out to the bakery, picked up some blueberry scones, and hurried back home. With a hot pot of coffee and bakery goods, Mom would could be held captive for hours.

Thirty minutes early, she bounced through the front door.

"Hi, babe!" She swished past me into the parlor and laughed. "Still sawing, I see."

"Yes. But I'm getting there." I grabbed her elbow and guided her to kitchen.

"Wait! I want to see all you've done!" she pulled away.

I took Mom on a quick routine tour of the house. I was trying to rush through it, but she wasn't going to have any of that. She meandered from room to room taking her time, inspecting every detail. I know how much she loved this old house, especially if there were any before-and-afters. Unfortunately, most of the before-and-afters were hidden in the walls, ceilings, or floors. Necessities like insulation, wiring, and beam supports weren't always the fun projects one can show off. But she seemed delighted in the few she could see, prompting suggestions for future projects, of course.

Back in the kitchen, Mom sat down while I served up the coffee and scones.

"Your voice mail sounded a little intense. Is it Meg? Is she all right? What did you find?" She ran it all together in an anxious tone.

"No, Mom, not Meg," I quickly reassured her. "She's fine. Really, she's great…perfect."

Although there were moments in my life that I wanted to keep private from my mother, Meg's welfare was never one of them. I was always upfront and honest when it came to Meg. Her granddaughter was her life, and together we shared it completely. I wanted Meg to be close to her grandparents with memories of complete joy. I was grateful that my mother's unconditional love gave her that joy every time. Her visits brought a glow to Meg's face. And vice versa.

"It's something I found in the house that belonged to Bertha, and I'm hoping you know something about it. I think it's pretty cool, but I'm not sure if there is really much of a story," I rattled. "Just hoping you can expand on it a bit, I guess."

I reached over one of the kitchen chairs and grabbed the large manila envelope from the counter behind me. As I pulled the paper out of the envelope, I could feel a tension in the room. Mom was quiet, and that was unusual. I slid the paper over to her across the table while continuously sipping my coffee and watching her face for any sign. But it never came. She stared at it for what appeared to be a millennium. I just kept sipping. Then I sipped some more. Finally, my frustration level piqued.

"Well, do you know anything about this?" I blurted impatiently. "Were you aware that she had written for one of the most liberal communist newspapers in Germany right before WWII?"

I leaned forward and cocked my head to put one ear closer, thinking perhaps that would prompt her to speak. With a calm, slow, and deliberate perpetual motion, she slid the paper back across the table and stuck it under my nose. She wasn't smiling. She wasn't frowning either, but her poker face was maddening. Finally, with a soft barely audible tone she simply stated, "Well, Eli, you know I can't speak or read German."

I was a little thrown back by this. I knew she couldn't speak or read German. She had mentioned it several times throughout the years. Just about every time Grandma had uttered something in German with a heavy peppering of Yiddish, Mom would simply wave her hands in the air, shrug her shoulders, and roll her eyes with a loud laugh. "Beats me, I have no idea what she's saying!" Her total lack of interest and curiosity surprised me and started to piss me off.

"I know you don't speak German, Mom," I emphasized sharply. "I have a translation of what the article is actually about, so I don't need for you to translate it to me."

I pointed at the date and impatiently tapped my finger on the year: 1927.

"I guess I'm trying to ask you about the fact that Grandma's little sis chose to hang out in Berlin pounding out movie reviews as the Nazis practiced their goose step up the streets!"

I spit out a little sarcasm. I could see that my mother wasn't appreciative of my inquisition which made me more determined. And suspicious.

"Mom, she wasn't just writing silly little movie reviews about romance or musicals," I continued in a softer voice. "After Hitler maneuvered himself into the position of prime minister of the Weimar Republic, things started getting really ugly in the streets, and the Jews were getting the brunt end. The German economy was at an all-time low, and tensions between the Gentiles and Jews began to heat up. He shut down the Weimar Republic and placed himself as Chancellor of Germany. Hence, his dictatorship began." I felt my face getting hot. "Also, he started cracking down hard on newspapers and any other media…" My voice started to fade off.

It was obvious I was the only one engaged in this conversation. I was losing hope of any additional help or information.

"I know my history, Eli," she scoffed and patted my arm, rising from the table.

Hell, a small bit of enthusiasm or interest from her would have been nice. She topped off our cups with the last of the coffee and started emptying the dish drain and putting dishes away. She knew something. Complete silence from my mother was never an option. And sharing stories of the past and history of relatives was always one of her favorite pastimes. Perhaps it was something so personal or difficult about Bertha that Mom just couldn't bring herself to say. Perhaps Bertha was communist. Maybe she was a spy! Whatever the story was, it wasn't like Mom to be biased and quiet. She championed for free speech and definitely supported Bertha no matter what she did or thought. So I let her do what she loved the most. I let her continue to clean my kitchen. She wiped up the counter—three times.

After a while she turned and said, "Where do you keep your coffee, honey? I'd like to make another pot if you don't mind."

I flopped back into my chair. Defeated, I reluctantly slid the newspaper back into the manila folder, stood up, and walked over to the pantry.

"Here ya go, Mom," I said, handing her the big tub of cheap coffee. "Would you like another scone?"

"No thanks, honey," she politely replied.

"You know, Mom, what she was doing was dangerous. As I said earlier, she wasn't just writing movie reviews." I emphasized quotations in the air with my fingers for dramatic effect. "This review was a direct jab at not only the pending evil of the Nazis but at the German population for not recognizing what was coming. I thought you would be really interested in a small part of her life that was actually quite remarkable, considering she turned out to be the little old cat lady in East Grayson, New Jersey." I ended on that note, knowing full well I had touched a nerve.

Although Mom never minded when the family teased about Great-Aunt Bertha, she had made it quite clear that a little teasing was one thing, but outright disrespect was quite another, and that wouldn't be tolerated. My intent was to stir emotion, and I could tell by her glare that it was working. I decided to stay quiet for a while and see if the uncomfortable silence would sway her.

After making another pot of coffee, she strolled over to the table, sat down, and said, "Let me see the translation, Eli?" I quickly opened the envelope and presented both the German and the English translation versions side by side.

"Here you go, Mom. I'll get us that cup of coffee while you read this. Take your time!"

After a few minutes, she looked up and said, "Yes, Bertie was a remarkable woman indeed, Eli."

For a few moments, she stared me in the eye with a smile of contentment that only confirmed that she knew much more about Bertha than she had ever told me. I got it. I had never asked her anything about Bertha before. My disinterest in the past had been loud and clear. I had no one to blame but myself.

"Mom, as a kid I just wasn't very interested in talking about any old person's life. I guess, now that I'm older and have a daughter, I want to know more about the person who left me this house. I want to be able to share it all with Meg someday. Please tell me more about her." I knew bringing her granddaughter into the mix would strike an emotional chord.

"Well, Eli, she had quite a life. She was one of the strongest women I have ever known and was, most definitely, my personal hero." She stared down at her coffee.

"Personal hero?" I leaned in closer. "Keep going!"

"Oh, Eli, it's a great story. But it's too long to get into now." She shook her head. "I have more newspapers that I have saved all these years," she continued, "and her journal. You are more than welcome to them."

"Yes!" I sat up. "Of course! And Penny knows a German language guy at the high school. He can translate any of it for us."

"Penny?" Her face lit up. She jumped on this like a flea to a dog's ass.

Damn it!

"Yeah, she's my neighbor across the street. I actually met her at that meeting you talked me into." I waved my hand swiftly as if wiping the chalkboard clean. "Aside from that, Mom, I can get all of Bertha's articles translated. Wouldn't that be cool to read them, to someday give them to Meg?" I talked fast trying to redirect the conversation off of Penny and back to Bertha.

"Thanksgiving is in a few weeks, Eli." She smiled and stood up, gathering her purse and keys. "After dinner and everyone has left, perhaps you and I can head to the attic, and I will share all I have saved in a large box," she continued as she walked to the door. "We can grab ourselves a little wine, and I'll tell you a wonderful story about Bertie and the people she loved so dearly." She stopped at the door. "It'll be fun!"

With her hand on my arm, Mom popped up on her toes and kissed me on the cheek. As she hurried down the sidewalk to her car, she waved, turned her head to the side, and shouted over her shoulder without looking back, "And you can share your story about Penny!"

Damn it.

8

Life is all memory,
except for the one present moment that goes by you so quickly
you hardly catch it going.
—Tennessee Williams

THE ATTIC IN our house had the same musty smell I remembered as a kid. It wasn't really a bad smell. It was just one of those smells that remains stored in your memory forever—like damp cardboard, stale beer, and muddy boots. And quite honestly, I was enjoying it while waiting for Mom to join me. Knowing her, it would take a while.

Mom was extremely social and couldn't pass through a room without engaging in conversations with every person in sight. Age or gender, none of it had any bearing on sparking her interest of the world. She loved people and always felt that everyone had a great story to tell. With each encounter, Mom would give her full attention to display empathy, praise, love, and interest. She was the best audience for the worst comedian. I admired her for having such a joyous and giving heart. I knew she had reserved many moments for me, and I probably wouldn't have made it through without her.

I was anxious to see what little mementos she had saved of Bertha's life and, most definitely, the news articles. So I tried to focus on the musty smell, dusty treasures, and silent game of *what's new* in the attic. As my eyes scanned about the dark A-framed perch, I began making a mental check of the familiar and not so familiar. My tricycle, skates, a box marked *Eli's Art,* and my small red wagon were scattered among the holiday crap. There were zipped up hanging closets of clothes that fit no one, a broken dirty fan, and some other forgotten piles of needful things. Although my childhood was plagued with painful experiences of bullying, the attic was a comforting reminder that I had had a wonderful childhood growing up with a safe and loving family.

My mother was gregarious, social, giving, and continuously involved in community and charitable events. Our middle-class comfort was never to be taken for granted. "What you are blessed with you share, Eli. When you feed others, you feed your own soul," she frequently reminded us. She took her own philosophies to heart and never deviated from what she knew was right and good.

But that wasn't to say my father wasn't just as giving and kind. His approach was just different. Quiet and unannounced, Dad was constantly running over to a neighbor's house helping with this or that. Most of it was emergent needs for those less fortunate. A broken water pipe or lack of heat would send him sailing out the door at all hours of the day or night, and he could be gone for hours. But the most impressive part of his giving was his decision to never verbally share stories or brag about the countless ways in which he helped make a difference in so many lives. And he never took money as payment.

I don't ever remember hearing him complain. I was the grateful beneficiary of that quiet demeanor. When I needed it most, Dad had the knack for reeling me in for our time in the garage. Our quiet tinkering and creating together fused our silent bond. He helped me to know when, where, and how I could defuse anger, sadness, and frustration. Because he reserved his words, few were aware of his intelligence. He was an avid reader, and it was rarely fiction.

Every Sunday we took a break, ate pretzels, and Dad would share some of the stories he had read, mostly biographies. Usually they were of men or women who had overcome great obstacles as children. But their ultimate outcome wasn't necessarily bonded to money or fame. For Dad, the greatest success stories were of those who gave back. They could have become billionaires. He gave them that. But if they were noted as being the founders of a great charity that changed the lives of others, then they took their rightful place in our garage during story time. I never saw him watching TV. And the only time he went to the movies was to take me. I never heard him yell or saw him angry. He was truly one of the most patient human beings I have ever known. While with him, I was never afraid, and I still missed him every day.

As my parents set positive examples throughout the community, they also took care of their own. My grandparents lived with us in their older years until my grandfather died. When my grandmother's dementia became so debilitating that we all feared for her safety, she was transferred to an assisted-living facility. My mother cried for weeks. First, there was the dangerous fall on the front porch. She survived that with only a few bumps and bruises. But when she started insisting that her food was being poisoned, we knew she needed more care than we could give.

Bertha was the only elder in my family who continued to live independently until she passed away. Since Mom called her every other day, it didn't take long for us to discover that Bertha had had a stroke early one morning in her own kitchen. When found, she was lying on the cold linoleum floor while a piece of burnt toast remained on the counter untouched. When the call came from Dad, I felt sad for him most of all. His bond with Bertha was strong. It was as though they belonged to a secret club where only the two of them ever got the jokes. Her needs were catered to immediately, and she'd always remained on the top of his list of priorities. I always felt she was odd. And of course, being old and living alone, it was obvious why Dad took such good care of her. Her odd physical gait had become a concern when she started wobbling more and banging into the side of furniture and door jams. After she had tripped on some throw rugs, Dad pitched anything that was deemed a dangerous obstacle. When walking together, he would gently take her by the elbow and patiently guide her along.

I spotted a few inherited objects from Bertha's house. Along with the mix of toys, clothes, and broken appliances, the attic had a spooky appearance like some of the oddity shops at Coney Island. Perhaps it was an indication that my parents had a hard time of completely letting go.

The attic even reminded me of the few good buddies of mine. We had been friends since kindergarten. As an only child, they were important to me and my salvation. We clung together through thick and thin in our secret club of outcasts. We had our own unique appearances. To the cruel cliquish kids, they were disfigurements that were meant to be feared and ridiculed.

My best friend, Josh, had bright-orange hair that swirled around his head in ridiculous cowlicks that peaked into devilish horns. With his massive freckles, the adults thought he was precious. To his classmates, however, he was nothing but a giant target. Their zings and darted words were hurtful. What they didn't know was that Josh struggled his entire short life to find his own sanctuary. He always appeared to be searching— to escape the beatings from his alcoholic father and the indifference of his codependent mother.

Right out of high school, Josh moved into an apartment and got a job at a tire repair shop. For a while, he appeared happy and content. But his own inner conflicts continued to surface with what his mother would whisper to friends and family as "gender issues." The toll on his sensitive inner core got the best of him. Finally, at twenty-four, he drove his jacked-up truck off a bridge late one Sunday night into the Passaic River. For years, his intentions that night were debated among friends and family. But knowing Josh, I was confident about how he was instrumental in his own demise.

After high school, there was an inverse relationship between his words and his actions. Less words appeared to bring more risks. And those close to him saw his daredevil antics becoming less humorous. He acted macho and indifferent. But our club knew better. He was fucked up and insecure in his own skin. The jacked-up truck, chain-smoking, and overabundance of alcohol sent red flags to everyone. But few talked of gender preferences back then, and he volunteered nothing to the contrary. It was the secret that so many in school either hid or shared in a whisper.

Navigating the hall, Josh would keep eyes forward with a deliberate gait. His focus was from point A to point B. I rarely saw the Josh that I knew until we were in our clubhouse, our sanctuary. And even then, the serious conversations were guarded. When cutting up with his best friends, he overcompensated for his *gender issues* with vulgar comments about the female anatomy. As adolescents, we were all crude and immature when it came to girls and their body parts. But Josh always seemed to show a sinister side and carried that well past his teens. Brief and volatile relationships with girls were always expected.

The realization that there wasn't much I could do to stop him was obvious. But the guilt has continued to haunt me with questions of how I could have intervened. I hadn't really thought of Josh in the last few years. My own struggles with a failing marriage, partial custody of Meg, and my poor attempt to stretch what little funds I had left kept me wallowing in my own self-indulgent pity.

Will, my other best friend and short for Wilbur, was another victim of the outcast boy's club. Fat at birth, Will's weight ballooned up and down his entire life. But his positive disposition, good humor, and general love for life was constant and carried him into a stable loving adulthood. Will never saw the drama. He always embraced the joy in everyone he met. Although teased relentlessly and cruelly for his weight, the words always appeared to roll off his chubby, dimpled shoulders. His own name, Wilbur, became a curse. He was likened to Wilbur the Pig in *Charlotte's Web*, hence, why he embraced the shortened version of Will. Later as young teens, we were required to read *Lord of the Flies*, which opened yet another can of worms. Being short and chubby, with round, thick glasses, set Will up for ruthless bullying. Shouted by some asshole, he was frequently subjected to "Hey, Piggy! I've got the conch!" The sting of those words were lost in the swarm of students between classes, allowing the coward anonymity and protection.

When asked why he always just laughed at such ruthless attacks, he simply replied, "Someday I'll be married, have children, and be a rich, happy fat man while the assholes will be miserable because they banked on appearances rather than value." To this day, Will is an extremely happy fat man. With a chubby wife and three chubby children, he lives in a large historical building in New York that he bought, renovated, and restored. Utilizing his architectural expertise and degree he gained from Yale, he is happy, successful, and very rich. He beat the assholes, after all.

Will was the buffer, liaison, and mentor of our kid's world. In our collective emotional embraces, Will ensured that Josh and I avoided the dark and insisted that we continuously strive for the light. It was when our lives took paths of their own, separated us via choices of educations, careers, marriages, and lifestyles, that we all lost touch. After Josh's death, Will and I made attempts to meet in NYC for an occasional lunch or drink. But with time and distance, those meetings became few and far between. Another regret of mine.

It was the sight of the little red wagon that brought memories to the surface. I stared at the rusty faded reminder of good and bad times. From the times we'd pushed, pulled, and rode that wagon as little guys inventing the wheel to the hysterically volatile teen years when it was used as our first ice cooler of beer in the wooden fort Dad and I had built together. It housed our club from boys to men. Mom hung on to that wagon as a memento of her little boy's childhood. But I snickered out loud, wondering if she would be so fond of that wagon if she only knew that Josh had used it as puke bucket one night out in the yard. Together, we had all discovered the dastardly effects of Jack and cola. Josh, of course, took it over the top and spent the night bent over the wagon. Remembering how hard we laughed that night I couldn't help but wonder, so I quickly I sneaked over for a sniff. The smell of Josh's puke was gone—years left out in the rain, I guess. At first, I laughed out loud at myself for braving the sniff test. But then again, I secretly wished I could sense a small part of Josh and that moment.

I was startled by the sound of footsteps coming up the attic ladder.

"Eli, come grab this!" Mom called from midway.

I slowly and carefully stood up, as not to whack my head on the rafters as I had seen Dad do so many times before. Bent over, I made my way to the steps and looked down through the hole to see Mom laughing out loud with a tray in hand and her face beaming up. As only my mother could do, she had created a tray of snacks.

"Mom, I just wanted a glass of wine!" I scoffed.

"Take the tray, Eli, and don't be a poo. This will be fun," she giggled.

Like Will, Mom was my other dark to light person. I grabbed the tray and smiled, despite myself. There were a couple of small clay mugs of beer and a giant warm pretzel to share.

I laughed. "Mom, we just had turkey dinner!" But I loved her for it. And her little pat on my back assured me that she knew how much I appreciated the memory of it all.

We settled down in two old camping chairs and clicked our mugs together.

"L'chaim," she said as she smiled and took a big gulp. As she bent down to place her mug on the floor, she picked up a large box and placed it on her lap. With a long, labored sigh, she placed one hand on top of the box and the other on my arm. "Eli, most of Bertie's life is in this box. Your dad was such a private person and talked very little about her life as a girl. Gosh, he never really talked much about his own life as you already know. I never felt it was my place to share any of this with you," she explained. "Secretly, I always hoped your dad would tell you the story. But he wouldn't. Maybe he just couldn't, Eli."

She gingerly pried off the lid as not to tear its old fragile frame and placed it on a shelf. The first piece of paper she handed me from the box was Bertha's birth certificate. Mom was starting at the beginning. I would be lying if I said I was thrilled. I didn't really want to know every small detail of Bertha's life as a child. I wanted to cut to the chase and get to the meat of the matter. I wasn't sure if there was enough beer in my mug for the long version. But Mom was leading this somewhere. So I quietly listened. And she told me the story—the story I *needed* to know.

9

In three words I can sum up everything
I've learned about life:
It goes on
—Robert Frost

H IRSH PLESSER AND Marie Ettinger were married March 6, 1882, in a synagogue in the small village of Skawina outside of Krakow, Poland. Only a few family members were in attendance, with a quiet reception immediately following the ceremony. Within a few hours, the newlyweds traveled a short distance to the modest family farm where they would make their home. On a small plot of land that Hirsh had inherited from his father stood an old two-story, wood-framed house. The small, white clapboard frame was in need of repair and remained sparsely furnished. But Hirsh and Marie were proud of their home, and as children of farmers, the newlyweds were knowledgeable and comfortable with living off the land as their ancestors had done for generations. Hirsh and Marie had known each other since childhood. Their marriage to one another had been considered by friends and family to be of a natural progression. Although neither possessed any formal education, they were well read, loved music, and were respected by their Jewish community as good, honest, and hardworking people.

In the second half of the nineteenth century, Skawina had become a railroad hub with one of the lines directly routed to nearby Krakow. With the railroad came new businesses and the small town flourished in an upward economic turn for the better. Hirsh and Marie's income came from selling farm goods at market as well as his part-time work on the section crew of the railroad. But regardless of a successful economy within the community, the young couple struggled, and it only became more difficult with time.

In 1900, Marie gave birth to their first daughter, Freida Edith Plesser. It was a long, difficult birth, and Marie never fully recovered. She was plagued with infections, fevers, and bleeding, inhibiting her ability to stand on her feet for long periods of time. Shortly after little Freida's birth, Hirsh was injured during a rail switch that left him permanently disabled in his left leg. When a cable snapped and plowed into a handful of men standing on the platform, the force of the whiplash killed two men, one of whom was decapitated. Although Hirsh was considered lucky to have survived the trauma, he continued to live with pain in his lower back, hip, and leg for the rest of his life. The lingering limp was severe and reduced his mobility to that of an old man. Marie's deteriorating health and Hirsh's injury began to take a toll on their ability to make ends meet.

Summers were spent preparing for the long, hard winters. Although she struggled, Marie continued to cook, can, sew, and nurture little Freida. However, once winter was in full force, the struggle to survive became more and more difficult. Deep ravines of snow, winds of gale force, and isolation bore down on them physically and emotionally. The cold, drafty house was void of heat save one iron potbellied stove in the kitchen supplied with chopped wood that Hirsh endlessly fueled to keep his family warm and dry during the bitter damp Polish winter months.

On February 15, 1905, Marie gave birth to her second child, Bertha Louise Plesser. Marie was already in her forties, and it had been five years since Freida had been born. Although doctors had assured her that another pregnancy was impossible, Marie's fluctuating hormones gave way to another baby girl. Marie was weak from constant bleeding, and fevers robbed her of strength and endurance. As well, baby Bertha was premature, small, and weak from hours of a difficult birth. Her tiny frame and immature lungs struggled for weeks to survive and her fragile condition was compromised further by the cold damp air. She rarely whimpered, and her mother's inability to nurse her left Bertha perpetually hungry and dehydrated.

Hirsh and little Freida worked throughout each day to save both mother and baby. A local midwife made as many visits as possible through the snow and wind, but there was little she could do and mostly depended on herbs and simple folklore practices to try and make Marie as comfortable as possible. As well, she attended to the needs of a tiny baby and a little girl to ensure they were fed and clothed while their father tended to fire wood, food, and their mother's critical needs. Finally, desperate to save his wife, Hirsh made the traumatic decision to take Marie to the nearest hospital in Krakow.

Although Krakow was only about twenty kilometers distance from Skawina, the journey in a wooden wagon with an old slow mare through treacherous snowbanks and blistering winds could take hours. The midwife supported this decision as Marie was hemorrhaging, and without immediate proper medical attention, she would not survive the next few days. The heartrending decision to leave his two small daughters with the midwife and his wife's condition overwhelmed Hirsh as he flopped into a kitchen chair and sobbed with his face buried in a dish towel. After a few moments, he wiped his face, stood up, and silently made his way to the back bedroom. It was the only time Freida had ever seen her father cry. Within the hour, Hirsh bundled up his wife and some supplies, such as blankets, food, and water, and carried Marie to the wagon.

For ten days the midwife and children heard nothing of Hirsh and Marie's status. Finally, in the dark, Hirsh returned alone. Freida was holding tiny Bertha while sitting by the potbellied stove when Hirsh entered the house. She would never forget the sound of her father's boots on the old wooden floor as they slowly and deliberately made their way down the long hall toward the kitchen. He entered the kitchen speechless. After a moment of looking at his daughters, he turned and left the room.

The midwife slowly turned back to the sink and continued scrubbing and rinsing the pots of the day. Freida could hear her soft sniffles and watched the back of her cry at the sink. The girls never saw their mother again and no discussion of her death was ever offered. At five years old, Freida had become a mother. She fed, clothed, rocked, and loved Bertha as the two grew up together. Freida would often refer to that time as the year she and little Bertha lost both parents.

10

Life is what happens to you
while you're busy making other plans.
—Allen Saunders

BERTHA STOOD AT attention in the middle of the hall, determined, with her eyes straight ahead. Like a miniature soldier, she was ready for inspection. Excited, she had difficulty standing still while Freida slowly and meticulously inspected every inch of her little sister's frame. Freida had personally seen to each detail of Bertha's first day of school preparation. From the tight single braid that hung down between her shoulders, accentuated by a small blue ribbon, to the tiny buttons on her shoes that could only be secured by a menacing hook, Freida had taken on the responsibility of Bertha, as always.

Four years earlier, Hirsh had sent his two daughters to live with his younger sister, Ruth, and her husband, Boris Michel, in Frankfurt, Germany. Poland's economic conditions began to deteriorate due to the 1901–1903 recession and the aftershocks of the Russo-Japanese War. By late 1904, over one hundred thousand Polish workers had lost their jobs. With mounting political tensions in Russia and Poland, Hirsh's financial instability worsened. His attempts to mask his physical pain with homemade vodka exacerbated his emotional fragility and made it impossible for him to care for his two small children.

It had been a year since Marie's death, and although he agonized over sending his daughters away, he knew he could no longer financially support them and secure their future in such a turbulent and dismal atmosphere. For his daughters to remain poor, oppressed, and uneducated was something he could not bear. His sister, Ruth, had met and married Boris Michel when she was fifteen years old. Boris was twelve years her senior and had already established himself as a merchant butcher for a small shop in Krakow, Poland. Immediately after marrying, Boris and Ruth moved to Frankfurt where Boris became an apprentice in his father's bakery shop. They took residence in a large flat above the store and inherited the business when his father died in 1902. Boris and Ruth monetarily fared well in the solid economy that Germany was enjoying, and the childless couple happily embraced the two girls into their home.

Moving into the small space with her aunt and uncle was an adjustment for Freida. She missed her father and the transition from farm land to city street felt confining and foreign. To her, Boris and Ruth were strangers. Until arriving in Frankfurt, Freida and Bertha had never met their aunt and uncle. Although their father had rarely spoken of his sister, it was usually in a kind manner. Ruth was a Polish Jew, and Boris was a German Catholic. Due to the increasing tensions between Germans and Jews during WWI, and leading up to WWII, Boris and Ruth quietly, without public display, worshiped in private. Very little attention to either religion or ceremony was ever displayed in their home. Prayer was to remain in the confines of their own room. What little Jewish prayer or ceremony that Freida could remember, she savored for the times when she and Bertha were in their room alone. Years later, Bertha would describe those moments in her journal as "a delightful time of religious invention."

The pain of parental separation haunted Freida for life. Throughout school, she rarely had friends or engaged in social activities outside her home. Although she was quiet and somber, she was kind, giving, and soft spoken. Bertha's well-being was Freida's quest and would remain so until they were both young adults. Together, they had sisterhood moments of giggles, sharing dreams, and a strong bond. They were able to communicate in silence, always knowing what the other was thinking and feeling.

Bertha was only one year old when her father sent her and Freida to Frankfurt. She had been too little to remember either of her parents. Since Freida was Bertha's only mother figure since birth, she adapted to the move quickly. Unlike Freida, Bertha was gregarious, joyful, and curious. Much to Freida's dismay, as Bertha grew, she could be constantly found engaged in conversation with complete strangers. She enjoyed helping in the bakery and mingling with customers. Although both girls were very intelligent, Bertha possessed a photographic memory. Her attention to detail far exceeded that of her peers and later allowed her to quickly excel in school. Even as a little girl, her memory skills allowed her to remember names, previous orders, billing numbers, and so on.

Her aunt and uncle welcomed her presence in the shop, but Freida was never too far behind watching and protecting. Although Bertha was bright, funny, and social, Freida hovered over her and fretted for Bertha's physical well-being. From the day she was born, Bertha struggled with physical abnormalities that, at first glance, were not immediately recognized. Her height placed her in the low end of a normal range for children her age. Therefore, she was frequently mistaken for a much younger child. As well, her arms and legs were too short for her elongated torso, giving her an awkward appearance. The poor range of motion in her joints caused difficulties in running, climbing, and other normal childhood activities. Throughout her life, she appeared slightly clumsy and uncoordinated. Her jerky movements and inability to maintain the same physical stamina and speed of her peers separated her from the other children and isolated her during times of play.

But whatever her physical deficits hindered, her personality and excelled intelligence made up the difference. She persevered in everything she attempted and never allowed herself to be left behind for long.

Like their mother, both Freida and Bertha read constantly. Their insatiable craving for books came at an early age. For Freida, her books of poetry and romance replaced real interactions with others and fed her never-ending desire to marry, have children of her own, and move to the United States. Little Bertha enjoyed adventure books. As she grew older, she plowed through history and biographical stories. Bertha often said that "the real stories were the best stories." She memorized dates, names, events, and would frequently quote famous historical figures. And even at the tender age of six, she announced to her family that someday she would be important, and her name would be in history books. In her teen years, she kept a journal of her readings, quotes, and her own adventures.

Eventually, both girls adjusted to their life with Boris and Ruth. They grew into young ladies who were respected by their peers and shown great love and encouragement at home. Boris and Ruth embraced their nieces, ensuring they received everything needed to develop into independent and educated young women. They were a happy family. But their comforts and sense of security would quickly fade.

From 1914 to 1918, Germany's involvement in WWI would prove to be an economic disaster for the country and its civilians. Due to the successful blockade by the British Navy, the German population experienced constant threats of starvation. Whatever few food rations remained were sent to the German troops fighting the war. As a result, the civilian population faced an extreme famine. To make matters worse, the massive military recruitment of German males left the country void of labor, including its agriculture. Potatoes were a staple in the German diet, and the lack of the potato crop forced the German population to seek alternative food sources. One crop that became prominent was the turnip. Because it had been typically used as an animal feed, the root vegetable was the only readily available crop left for consumption. Although turnips were used in every kind of food possible to feed civilians and wounded soldiers returning home, malnourishment and illness claimed thousands of lives.

The devastation between 1916 and 1917, what would be called the *Turnip Winter*, severely affected the morale of the German people. Their stomachs weren't used to eating turnips. Unlike the small tender variety more suitable for humans, the turnip crop used for livestock was large and tough. Consuming large quantities of the cruciferous root caused great stomach distress, mostly in the form of severe diarrhea or bloating; all of which accelerated their already compromised malnutrition. Boris and Ruth did all they could to keep food available for their family of four. Freida and Bertha helped bake dried turnips into bread. As a bakery, they were well stocked with grains and other dried goods for a while. For fear of looters or government confiscation, they stockpiled what little they had left in a secretly vaulted door in the back of a linen closet. Along with stored preserves and other candied fruits and nuts, their family was able to fare better than most. But in time, the shelves grew thin, as did their bodies.

Meanwhile, back home in Poland, approximately two million Polish troops fought with the three occupying powers of Germany, Austria-Hungary, and Russia. There were devastating losses of lives, and several thousand Polish civilians were moved to labor camps in Germany. Germany found itself filled with prisoners. Internment camps spread out in the countryside and nearby towns. French, Russian, British, American, Canadian, Belgian, Italian, Romanian, Serbian, Portuguese, and Japanese were crammed into spaces of less than twenty-six square feet per prisoner. Overcrowding worsened the already poor conditions lending to an epidemic of cholera. Many of the *camps* were nothing but tents where prisoners dug holes to keep warm. Hangars, old forts, schools, barns, and various other types of shelters were used. In February 1915, there were approximately 625,000 prisoners housed in these various camps. By October 1918, the prisoner population swelled to 2,415,000. But even in the best of shelter situations, including military and civilian, the deaths were estimated at well over one million.

Hirsh Plesser was among the Polish civilians that had been moved to the Holzminden Internierungslager labor camp in the outskirts of Lower Saxony, Germany. This camp existed from 1914 to 1918 and housed up to ten thousand civilians of enemy states. Due to his already fragile physical condition, Hirsh died in the winter of 1916. The exact date was never established, and no death certificate was ever presented. His name was simply listed on a public notice on the door of the German National Library in Frankfurt. It took six months for the girls to receive news that their father had perished during the Russian invasion.

At the end of WWI, Boris struggled to bring the bakery back into the thriving business it had once been. But Germany's economy never fully recovered after the war. The country was forced to pay large reparations to France and Great Britain under the rules of the Versailles Treaty. As well, foreign countries placed protective tariffs on German goods, disallowing Germany the ability to make the necessary income. As an attempt to compensate, Germany began printing large amounts of money. For a brief time, things appeared to improve, and Boris and Ruth were able to sell small amounts of baked goods to a few customers. Over time, however, the excess of money sent Germany's economy into a hyperinflation. Millions of German marks became worthless.

Through it all, Boris and Ruth continued to send the girls to school. Freida became tall and pretty and remained quiet and shy. As a young woman, she spent most of her free time alone. She met a fellow student, Carl Henich. He was a soft-spoken young man who displayed a kind and gentle demeanor. Both were serious students and became fast friends. In 1920, they married and took jobs teaching in a neighborhood school. Boris had cleared out a small utility space in the back of the store where Freida and Carl could stay until the economy improved and they could establish their own home. With Boris's permission, Carl rebuilt old furniture and shelves and created a nice space for his new bride. Carl and Freida's income, albeit small, brought more financial stability into the house.

When done with her daily classes, Bertha worked at a part-time job typesetting in a local print shop. While there, she became increasingly intrigued by the articles that were printed each day and sent out to local independent papers. Many of the articles addressed the political and economic atmosphere in Germany as well as in Europe. Bertha read every article and savored each name and date. What words and context she didn't understand were saved until dinnertime when she could ask Uncle Boris. And although her journal was filled with the entries of any young girl, such as daily routine, feelings, and dreams, it also included detailed accounts of the disturbing events that unfolded before her. Her journal would prove to be a valuable document of Bertha's life journey as well as its historical value.

11

Life isn't about finding yourself
Life is about creating yourself
—George Bernard Shaw

A
T TWENTY-ONE, SHE was doing exactly what she had always planned. She was living on her own in Berlin, making new friends, and had landed her first real job. As copy editor for the *Die Rote Fahne,* Bertha gained her first true sense of independence. Carl and Freida had eventually moved to London. Ultimately, their goal was the United States. For Bertha, however, her decision to live in Berlin was an easy one. She knew where and how she wanted to live. Boris and Ruth stayed in the bakery and rented the small back room to a young couple. Business was improving, and they benefited from the rent and increased sales.

Between 1925 and 1933 a housing project had been completed and was a milestone in urban housing. Bertha was thrilled at her new small space. The Hufeisensiedlung, Horseshoe Estate, was designed by architect Bruno Taut, a committed socialist and utopian architect. Germany's population had doubled during the turn of the century and continued to do so about every twenty-five years. The country was beginning to enjoy a Golden Twenties–era boosting industrialization and, with it, a population explosion. Swiftly, Berlin's residents grew to 3.8 million, and it became the third largest metropolis, following New York City and London. Hence, the need for efficient affordable housing became critical.

Her first apartment in the Hufeisensiedlung was nothing short of a personal triumph in her eyes. The complex was shaped in a *u*, hence the name. Although a huge complex, it seemed warm and cozy due to its design of beautifully bright colored doors and windows. Taut had designed each interior apartment with minimalistic style and furniture, relying on the colors as its art. Gardens were placed close to the front doors of the apartments in outdoor common areas maintained by all residents, where fresh vegetables could be grown in a cooperative manner.

Bertha's apartment was a small flat with a bathroom, which housed a toilet, tub, and a coal-fired water heater. It provided her with an efficient kitchen equipped with a sink, gas cooker with two burners, and a small cupboard. Her flat provided a separate bedroom, in which Bertha rarely slept. She had shared a bedroom with Freida her whole life and found it difficult to sleep alone. Frequently, she fell asleep on a small chaise in the living room. There were two benefits to this accommodation: it reduced her loneliness for Freida, and it was warmer there close to the fire. The more expensive flats at Hufeisensiedlung were provided with central heating in what was known as the *sixth section*. Bertha's only heat came from a coal oven in the living room. This didn't seem to bother her as she had written her sister about the beautifully colored glazed tiles that shimmered in the flickering light of the coals in the dark, calming her and enabling her to drift into a "dreamlike fairy tale."

She missed Freida terribly but remained in constant communication writing to her every day. Visiting would be next to impossible. The trip departing Berlin and arriving in London at Liverpool Street arrived after a stop in Holland and a ferry to Harwich completing a grueling six-day journey. Bertha's funds wouldn't provide for such extravagance. As well, things were heating up in Europe and traveling held risks that put people ill at ease for anything considered leisure. Letters to Freida were kept light and simple. Political activities or opinions never entered the paper trail. Names of friends, the contents of her newspaper articles, or other bits of information that may draw attention to herself, or those she knew, were deliberately void of mention. But it wasn't necessarily for her own protection. She was aware of how volatile it was to be writing for a communist newspaper such as *Die Rote Fahne*. She wanted to protect Freida, Boris, and Ruth. So she documented everything she could in her journal and saved her opinions for her corner of the newspaper.

The *Die Rote Fahne*, aka *Red Flag* or the *Flag of the Revolution*, was a communist paper that began in the 1800s. In 1920, its circulation was close to 30,000. By 1932, it swelled to an impressive 130,000. Its turbulent and dangerous history led it to be secretly distributed by its members, mostly to the workers at the factories with the remaining going to residential areas.

Like most newspapers, it offered sections of interest and was written in easily understandable language allowing simple comprehension for workers trying to learn much of the Marxist theory. Included were such sections as Tribune of the Proletarian Woman, the Working Woman, Economic Review, and For the Proletarian Youth. Before 1933, the title page often displayed political caricatures, awarding the newspaper the historical significance of its time. Such designs were artistically contributed by illustrators Helen Ernst, George Grosz, and John Heartfield.

Bertha Plesser's contributions came in the section titled Proletarian Films, and in 1927, she wrote her first film review of the much-anticipated *Metropolis*. Although it opened with mixed reviews, Bertha was mesmerized by the giant skyscrapers and machines. Her favorite was the telephone in which the caller could hear and see the person on the other end. But the message she most wanted to convey was the story—a protected and sheltered son who rebels against his father, a capitalist of the cruelest convictions in an isolated world of privilege. Her observations of the struggles and mistreatment of the poor laborers of her own country haunted her, and she saw *Metropolis* as nothing short of visionary.

Bertha frequently referred to her short time at *Die Rote Fahne* as "my beginning." She felt alive there and knew in her heart that what she was doing was important, mindful, and necessary. Her admiration for one of the founders of the newspaper, Rosa Luxemburg, helped her to stay strong and push all fears to the back of her mind. Although she had never met Luxemburg, Bertha wrote frequently about her in her journal. Details of Luxemburg's writings were of special interest due to their political nature. As well, she admired her as a political activist, socialist theorist, feminist, and teacher.

Luxemburg paved an important yet dangerous path for many. In 1919, her assassination in broad daylight in the streets shocked those who knew and respected her work. But when her corpse surfaced in the Berlin Landwehrkanal, she became an icon for the importance of the free press represented in *Die Rote Fahne,* et al. That same year, cofounder Karl Liebknecht was also assassinated and the two share adjoining tombs in Berlin. It was in their building that Bertha worked for the *Die Rote Fahne* and she felt honored to be a part of the movement that was clearly designed for the factory workers and women. As well, anti-Semitism was growing quickly, and the division in the population became more apparent each day. Whistles and sneers from young German men often taunted employees as they entered the building for work.

Bertha stayed close to those sympathetic to the causes of which the newspaper kept focus. She felt safe there. But her youth and naivete would prove to hinder her better judgment in the days and months to come. Although most days she felt empowered, happy, focused, and energized, there were days when she truly felt as though she was alone, vulnerable, and in over her head. No longer did she seek conversations with strangers as she so enjoyed as a child. It became increasingly difficult to determine friends or foes. However, she was part of the team that distributed the papers daily and enjoyed the few encounters with those like-minded people who appeared grateful for the paper.

She knew writing for the *Die Rote Fahne* was a risk. But, in her heart, it was a necessary risk. As a gregarious social being, she found it difficult to contain herself at times. But she quickly learned that her best strategy would be one of furtive approach. So she tucked her Star of David necklace deep into her blouse and rarely spoke of her background. Her short stature allowed her to duck her head in crowds and remain anonymous. She had made just a few friends at the apartments and kept close to those at the newspaper. She visited Boris and Ruth less and less, attempting to protect them from her activities with the paper. She looked forward to the day when everything was right again.

12

Friendship marks a life even more deeply than love
Love risks degenerating into obsession,
friendship is never anything but sharing
—Elie Wiesel

BERTHA WAS EXCITED about the visiting journalist coming to the *Die Rote Fahne*. Marcus Sindel was well known throughout Germany as well as Europe. He had been writing at the *Frankfurter Zeitung* for over a decade. Although his political articles were based on factual events and people, some found him too opinionated and brash. But his unabashed approach to journalism was highly respected by the members of the resistance. And he was there for a purpose. He explained his goals and objectives to no one. His cocky persona and arrogant approach intimidated many. But his focus remained necessary, to follow and bring forth the work of Rabbi Leo Baeck in a show of solidarity.

Sindel's camaraderie with Rabbi Baeck created empowerment for Baeck's following, and the *Die Rote Fahne* was anxious to cover all their activities to boost the morale of the resistance. The safety in numbers approach was the main operative plan and Sindal hoped to eventually spread that empowerment back to Frankfurt as quickly as possible.

Leo Baeck was president of the union of German rabbis. He had become a leading Rabbi in Berlin, and it was estimated, at the time, that about one-third of the German Jews lived in Berlin. During WWI, he centered himself at the front and preached to members of all faiths. Soldiers and civilians alike respected him, and he gained a huge following. The rising Nazi organization found him to be a threat, and although Baeck had numerous opportunities to leave Germany, he insisted upon staying.

Nazi influence began to refer to all German Jews as "Jews of Germany" to diminish their coexistence as people of German heritage. This helped broaden support for the expulsion of Jews from the German community. It was a clear indication that anti-Semitism was heating up with an exponentially fast and powerful momentum. Baeck belonged to, and represented, several organizations, and he was frequently sought after for speaking at universities and events. He dedicated his time to boosting the morale of the Jewish population as well as diminishing their persecution. And when necessary, he was instrumental in aiding to their emigration from Germany. Writing for the *Die Rote Fahne* in Berlin afforded Marcus Sindel the perfect arena for his coverage of Leo Baeck. When asked how long he planned on staying at the newspaper, Sindel would slightly smile and respond, "As long as it takes."

Meanwhile, Bertha's admiration and respect for Marcus grew at a fast and furious rate. While some resented his arrogance, she respected his serious dedication and was physically drawn to his confidence. He was smart, and she admired his work ethics. But she was attracted to his appearance as well. He was handsome, tall, and lean, with a thick mop of dark, curly hair. Although his expression appeared to be in a constant stance of concern, his eyes were soft and gentle. As the weeks progressed, she found herself totally absorbed in his every move. She told herself, and others, that they were merely friends. But it quickly became obvious to all around them that Bertha and Marcus were growing close.

He, too, was equally drawn to Bertha. He enjoyed the attention she gave him, and although she remained professional and serious in her work ethic, he relished her joy and humor. Her ability to make him laugh kept him nearby. As well, their flirtatious banter, when no one was looking, instigated a fun game that allowed them to occasionally escape the too often morbid mood of the office. They began spending a great deal of time together outside of the newspaper.

Although they refused to hide their friendship and respected camaraderie as journalists, Bertha and Marcus kept their visits private outside of work. Together, they shared long walks in parks, dinners, and movies. But Bertha's favorite moments were the quiet ones. Evenings with wine, music, and long conversations about the paper, writing, and what was consistently on everyone's mind, the resistance. She was one of the few people that ever saw the loose joyfulness of Marcus. The Marcus who could spontaneously burst into laughter, often over something humorous Bertha had said. They seldom discussed religion. It wasn't deemed necessary. He was an Orthodox Jew, and she knew that ties to home were strong. But his reference to his family and friends in Frankfurt were frequently aligned with the name Anna. That confirmed Bertha's fear that his heart was already taken elsewhere.

At the paper, Bertha was readily at hand to help Marcus with research, typing, editing, or running copy. For the most part, she was happy to do so as it kept her close to him and in the constant contact she was starting to crave. She loved writing for the *Die Rote Fahne*, but she was beginning to tire of movie reviews and the general feeling of isolation from the rest of the paper. She felt as though her contribution wasn't taken as seriously as many of the other sections and referred to her spot in her private journal as "my little corner of the paper." Although she was well read in history, she was young and had much to learn about the psychological makeup of societies. For the most part, in her eyes, movies were still seen as predominantly just entertainment. Her recent exposure to the impact that film could have on a society, and vice versa, was beginning to expand and she wanted to soak up as much as possible.

New genres of film were popping up everywhere in Germany. The film industry was growing at a faster rate than theaters could accommodate. From 1920 to 1933, Germany produced films that would be revered globally into the twenty-first century and set standards for filmmakers that would change the course of film forever.

Die neue Sachlichkeit (New Objectivity) frequently depicted the despair of the German people following WWI. Such movies as *Ritual Murder* (1919), *Joyless Street* (1925), *The Loves of Jeanne Ney* (1927), and *Pandora's Box* (1929) injected anti-Semitism and xenophobia into the storylines. As well, *Kammerspiel* (Chamber Drama) films were known as *Instinct*. This genre focused more on the psychological intimacy of its characters and centered around people of lower-middle-class status. State director and film producer Max Reinhardt was best known for these films and carried his expertise from Germany to the United States where he expanded his career into theater schools throughout the 1930s until his death in 1943 in New York.

Popular genres such as nature films, or *Bergfilm*, introduced great experimentation in technology and animation. However, the most innovative technology of all was sound. It transformed film in a direction never seen or heard before, and the world of filmmakers were feverishly experimenting with its very existence. Most notably was *The Blue Angel* (1930), directed by Josef von Sternberg and produced by Erich Pommer. It was Germany's first *talkie* and considered to be one of the first sound films in the world. Shot in several versions, utilizing several soundtracks in both German and English, it became a huge success of both the film and its star, Marlene Dietrich, in the United States.

The result of the explosive film industry brought a new addition to newspapers: film critics. Rudolf Arnheim of *Die Weltbühne,* Béla Balázs *of Der Sichtbare Mensch,* Siegfried Kracauer of *Frankfurter*

Zeitung, and Lotte H. Eisner of *Filmkurier* were the most prominent and respected. They helped to bring controversial social issues to the surface and encouraged public debate on anti-Semitism, prostitution, and homosexuality.

Political satire made its way into the art world after WWI and continued until the end of WWII. Prominent artists such as George Grosz and Otto Dix embraced two movements, Dada and New Objectivity (*Neue Sachlichkeit*), both of which were a direct reaction to the post-WWI trauma and societal difficulties incurred by the war. As well, they addressed the pending war that would follow and its embrace of Adolf Hitler. Grosz was arrested for blasphemy after his widespread publication of *Shut Up and Keep Serving*, depicting Christ on a cross donning a gas mask. The charge was later dismissed when a judge deemed the drawing as more of a stance against militarism than religion. Otto Dix's work attacked the corrupt and immoral German society in such works as *Seven Deadly Sins* in 1933.

Art museums and films became the date of choice for Marcus and Bertha. Often, they were horrified, angered, and yet inspired by the social implications of what they had just seen, read, viewed, and absorbed. For Bertha, each new exhibit or film prompted discussion that was infused with debate, retelling, reiterating, and a craving to learn. Her friendship with Marcus quickly evolved into that of a mentorship. Marcus was ten years older than Bertha, and he appeared worldlier to her than men her age. Bertha was still a child only nine years old during WWI, while Marcus had served at the tender age of nineteen. She quickly recognized that knowing *of it* was years away from being *in it*. She memorized their discussions and transposed them into her journal every day. He frequently reminded her of her importance and contribution to the paper. He openly marveled at her ability to memorize even the most minute detail. But he warned her that although remembering facts was an imperative tool for building the foundation, without analysis and critique, the facts would simply become nothing but regurgitation, void of their importance. He taught her how to see openly and recognize what was going on around her, why it was happening, and what it all meant. He showed her good journalism, good friendship, and ultimately, good sex.

13

Appear weak when you are strong,
and strong when you are weak
—Sun Tzu

EFORE THE DISCOVERY of intimacy, Bertha was able to keep her emotions in check. With each physical encounter, her struggle became greater. Sex changed everything for Bertha. Her feelings for Marcus quickly moved from the feeling of a schoolgirl crush to a deep love. Often, Marcus spent the evening at her apartment. Rarely did he stay until morning. She felt a pang of sadness each time he left before dawn. Although she convinced herself that their relationship must be kept private due to the volatile times in which they lived, she worried that she was just trying to convince herself of something that didn't exist between them. As well, the pending possibilities of Anna in Frankfurt tormented Bertha. Marcus rarely mentioned Anna's name anymore, and Bertha was forever hopeful that it might be a sign of him letting her go. But frequently he appeared aloof, as if all thoughts were elsewhere. The more he pulled away, the more she felt anxious and unsure.

Marcus had perfected the art of compartmentalizing his emotions, and Bertha was frustrating. Professionally, he ended every project before beginning a new one. And once ended, it wasn't to surface again until *he* was ready. This carried over into his personal life as well. She started feeling as if she were one of those projects and, frequently, was tucked away neatly until thought of again. When the pressure got too great, she would gingerly hint of her anxiety for their future together, or lack thereof.

But Marcus ended the conversations abruptly and reminded her of the dangerous times that surrounded them. "Don't go too deep with us," he would say tenderly, "We might not have control of our future." But it was too late. She was deep. She was deeper than she even knew.

Since the 1929 economic crash in the United States, Germany was in constant turmoil. The repercussions weren't felt immediately. But large waves of devastating economic events were swift and merciless. When the Versailles Treaty failed, Germany agreed to the Dawes Plan of 1924 after much debate, reducing the payments and inhibiting restructuring of its borders. The five nations representing this plan were the United States, United Kingdom, Italy, Belgium, and France. Germany would be given fifty-nine years to pay off a debt of billions of German marks. At the time, the United States was viewed as the richest nation in the world. On the committee of the Dawes Plan were large banks with even larger names, such as J. P. Morgan. The hope was to boost the economy of a stronger independent Germany and structure profitable trade between the two countries, all the while keeping USSR's communism at bay. As well, the United States continued to make loans to Germany to ensure its success.

Financially, all appeared to be going well. The United States was enjoying the *Roaring 20s* and Germany's high life was known as the *Golden Years*. But this all came to a screeching halt with the stock market crash in New York. Germany had become economically dependent upon loans from the United States as well as exportation of goods in a trade agreement. When the loans ended and trade sanctions were imposed, Germany could no longer benefit from the prosperity it had enjoyed for five years. The *Golden Years* were deemed as artificially induced, and Germany dramatically felt the repercussions of its loss. As companies closed and banks shut down, unemployment exploded. The German people were losing faith in the Weimar government. Heinrich Bruning, chancellor of Weimar Republic in 1930, responded fearfully to inflation and the encroaching budgetary deficits. His tragic decision to increase taxes and implement wage cuts exacerbated the unemployment catastrophe.

It had been two years since Carl and Freida had sailed for America. Bertha desperately missed her sister but took great comfort in knowing they were safe. The frequency of their communication to each other diminished greatly since Freida's move. But they persevered and Freida's most recent letter gave Bertha great comfort. Carl had family in New Jersey, which made it easier for the couple to settle. They were living with his aunt in a large farmhouse which helped with their expenses. Freida was able to continue to teach. Carl had secured carpentry work and, in time, had made quite a name for himself as a skilled artisan carpenter. Before the crash, he was hired throughout New Jersey and New York, creating and building beautiful wood work that adorned the architecture of many elite homes. They were frugal people. But Freida was suspicious of banks and businesses. So the bulk of her earnings went into a box securely hidden in the floor planks of their bedroom. She told no one of this, and Carl never understood how she was able to provide so well on their meager salary during the Depression.

To keep men working, President Franklin D. Roosevelt established the Civilian Conservation Corps (CCC) in April of 1933. The program was federally funded and aided in putting thousands of Americans to work during the Depression. Since the programs were stationed in federal and state parks, the focus for their existence was environmental. Forestry management practices were introduced as well as the building of roads, bridges, shelters and trails. Many of the ranger stations at the parks were built by the CCC and required skilled carpenters.

Carl was hired as part of a team called *Local Experienced Men*. His job was to teach the carpentry and building skills necessary to the young men working at the designated CCC parks. Typically, they earned thirty dollars a month. Since their room, board, and medical care were included with the job, they could keep five dollars of their monthly salary and send the remainder home to help support their families.

Carl and Freida's stability was a tremendous relief to Bertha. However, Bertha's surroundings became more and more fearful. The streets were filled with pandemonium and lawlessness, and the continued turmoil was clearly sending a message of discontent. Not having to worry about her sister, Bertha was able to focus on herself. Regardless, her future was ambiguous.

By the fall of 1932, over half of Germany's industrial production halted. Within a year, over six million people were unemployed. Germany's children suffered from malnutrition and thousands had died. As a result, German voters began to view mainstream political parties as inefficient and detrimental. They began to seek alternatives that were radical, causing instability within the parties. Adolf Hitler began to clearly define the primary goal of the Nazi party—to secure *lebensraum* (living space) for the Aryan master race. Political discord, fear, and hunger set the perfect stage for the Nazi party's rise in the general election in March. Just a few months earlier, the Reichstag Parliament building had burned down, and the blame was placed on the Communist Party. Once the KPD was banned, the Nazi party became the majority and the domino effect of ethnic cleansing began.

The Enabling Act was passed March 23, 1933. Without necessity of the approval from the Parliament, Hitler created his own governmental laws. Within a couple of months, the Nazi Secret police, aka the Gestapo, was formed, and the Nazis oversaw local government. Germany was no longer a democratic state. Adolf Hitler was in charge, and a dictatorship was born. His first act of business was the elimination of trade unions. Trade unions were seen as communist and socialist by Hitler, and therefore he set out to minimize the working man's power. Supporting the Nazi agenda of a racist and pro-corporate platform, employers and workers were stripped of all rights. Any collective bargaining and right to strike were outlawed. All pay and working conditions would be the decision of Hitler and his officials. Wages were immediately frozen, and all Jews were banned. Any dissension by employer or worker was immediately impeded with the arrest of the offender. Many were often tortured and immediately sent to concentration camps.

The atmospheric discord in the streets and in the papers worried Marcus, and he began to fear for his family in Frankfurt. His attendance at the paper diminished greatly as he busied himself attending rallies and speeches. News came that Anna's father had been arrested at the IG Farben chemical plant in Frankfurt. No longer was Marcus's focus on the *Die Rote Fahne,* and Bertha could sense his emotional pull was elsewhere. She was troubled with her own state of being, and it was engulfing her every moment.

Bertha hadn't felt well for weeks and appeared to be losing weight. She tried to dismiss the possible causes of her condition, but when a local midwife confirmed the status of Bertha's pregnancy, she was overwhelmed with fear. On several occasions she attempted to approach Marcus. But her fear and lack of self-assurance hindered her ability to confide in him. When Marcus announced his immediate plans to return to Frankfurt, Bertha's desire to divulge her condition was gone. Internally, she continually debated and questioned their relationship. On the surface, they were great friends and lovers. They had laughed and loved—and often. But the laughter was waning. And they hadn't loved in weeks.

The lack of laughter and sex was justified and excused. She justified that his ability to act aloof was nothing more than a reaction to the turbulent times. He was focused on Rabbi Baeck, the paper, the Communist Party, the Revolution, the failing economy. But down deep in her churning gut, she knew. She knew that if he had truly fallen in love with her, he would have said the words, taken her hand, led her through it all together. He wouldn't be leaving her behind: he would take her with him. Her reality was not what she had always hoped. She had fooled herself. She had fooled herself about Germany, the success of the Revolution, and Marcus. And she had sadly discovered that she had fooled herself about her own physical condition.

With Carl and Freida so far away and Marcus leaving, Bertha was starting to panic. She was a single pregnant Jewish woman in Nazi Germany. And she was alone.

14

Every man has his secret sorrows which the world knows not;
and oftentimes we call a man cold when he is only sad.
—Henry Wadsworth Longfellow

THE GERMAN POPULATION was quickly surrendering to its fears and anxieties of communist influences. This stirred the perpetual pot of racism, xenophobia, homophobia, and sexism. As a result, the implosion of civil liberties and democracy easily cleared the way to political measures that served Hitler's agenda for a superior Germanic race.

The efficiency of hindering the mass media through censorship and propaganda spread a clear and swift message from the new regime of what would and would not be tolerated. The Nazis were dictating how radio, press, and newsreels were to spread the fear quickly and became the priority of solidifying support for the regime through propaganda. In the winter of 1933, there were 4,700 newspapers in circulation. The Nazis only controlled three percent of them and wanted more. Rudolf Mosse, August Scherl, and Leopold Ullstein were the three largest publishing houses in Berlin. All three had been well established since the 1800s and were known as liberal powerhouses of the Berlin newspaper district.

August Scherl's publication, *Berliner Lokal-Anzeiger*, was one of the first newspapers in Germany to fund itself through advertising. After WWI, however, Scherl's publishing house experienced rising financial hardships which left it vulnerable. Eventually, it was taken over by Alfred Hugenberg in 1916. Turning it into a nationalist publication, Hugenberg became a vehicle for Hitler's rise to power.

Another target and focus of concern for the Nazis was a large advertising agency that was owned by the Mosse family. Started by Rudolf Mosse, the family continued to run the company via his grandson, George L. Mosse. Eventually, it transformed into the *Berliner Tageblatt*. Known for publishing many of Berlin's liberal papers, it had an abundant and thriving circulation. The liberal editor-in-chief, Theodor Wolff, would later become the namesake for Germany's prize for journalism. Hitler publicly denounced the Mosse enterprise and shut its doors. Fearing imprisonment or death, the Mosse family fled Germany the day Hitler took power. Later, as a professor at the University of Wisconsin, George Mosse published more than two dozen books addressing fascism, and in 1998, he was awarded the prestigious Leo Baeck Medal.

One of the largest well-known publishing houses was Berlin's daily *Vossische Zeitung*. Family owned as well, the Ullsteins employed over ten thousand people. In accordance with the 1933 *Schriftleitergesetz* (Editor Law), journalists not deemed as racially and politically reliable were banned from employment. In just a few months, Nazi sympathizers marched through the Ullstein offices, chanting and threatening employees. The Ullsteins were intimidated into leaving. Ultimately, they sold all of their assets for only 15 percent of its worth.

These powerful actions set in motion a panic that spread quickly throughout the newspaper industry and was responsible for large numbers of reputable journalists' swift exit from the country.

The Nazi message to the media community was swift and calculated. As well as economic strategies and financial takeovers, the storm troopers (SS) took to the streets and physically began cleaning house. As they swept through the offices of politically opposing parties, printing presses and newspapers were destroyed with disregard. Through the new Reich Press, the Propaganda Ministry assumed control and began strict guidelines that would ensure regulation of the media and a purge of undesirables. The new Editors Law of 1933 would forever exclude Jews as well as their spouses from the profession of German journalism during the Third Reich. Those accused of failing to adhere to the new policy would be sent to concentration camps. When the dust settled, the number of newspapers had dwindled from a healthy 4,700 to a paltry and controlled 1,100.

On the few days Bertha was present for these intrusions, she kept her head lowered at her desk. This posture had become the norm for her. The once vivacious and joyous girl had slowly been reduced to quiet, somber, and socially secluded within herself. To draw attention to herself was dangerous. But her lack of interaction and joy felt like death. She began to spend less and less time at the paper. She knew that less time there protected her from the Nazi intrusions that were becoming more frequent. She had seen employees harassed and removed. Once, the SS stopped her at the entrance door and demanded to see her papers and ID. As she was fumbling in her bag, the soldiers were distracted by a panicked young man darting out the building and into the street. Free of the harassment, she turned and scurried down the street in the opposite direction. A few blocks away, she turned the corner and vomited in a stairwell. She never returned to work.

Unfortunately, not checking in meant not getting paid. Often, for hours, she would sit in the nearby park on a bench by the pond. A cup of hot tea settled her stomach and temporarily diminished her hunger. Staring down at the shadows of the trees on the sidewalk, she took solace at the ever-changing shapes created as the sun made its way across the sky. She knew that time changed many things physically and emotionally and it was changing her, changing her body, her life, her heart.

The glimmering crystal reflection of sun on the pond was mesmerizing. And the mother duck with her playful ducklings splashing about provided a moment in a vacuum, void of the outside, of fear, pain, hunger, or decisions. It was her sanctuary full of nothing but void.

Although businesses, media, and the overall economic atmosphere of Germany unfolded under Hitler's plan, an even darker and more sinister plan had begun. It was the selection of desired heritable characteristics to improve future generations. Eugenics. Although globally the topic of eugenics wasn't new and had been explored and debated throughout human history, the interpretation and implementation of eugenics before and after Hitler created a unique transformation that would be considered one of the most horrific master plans in human history.

During the nineteenth century, a steady decline in the birthrate produced, on average, only one child per German family. Berlin was considered a culturally sophisticated city and had produced the lowest birthrate of any capital city in Europe. Germany's Constitution outlawed abortion and upheld a prison term for both the woman and the doctor involved. Later, during the Weimar Republic, a court's decision legalized abortion, but only in cases of danger to the life of the mother. Between 1920 and 1930, the Weimar Republic periodically debated the liberalization or the legalization of abortion. Ultimately, abortion continued to remain illegal, although the punishment was reduced from a felony to a misdemeanor.

A great deal changed during Hitler, however. In 1933, a law forbidding abortion to Germans was reintroduced with heavy penalties. After WWI, there was a shortage of men. Once again, Germany began to experience a low birth rate. This concerned the Nazis, as their mission for world power with a robust military would require a large population of strong males. Therefore, German women were pressured to bear as many children as they could, all for the sake of the Reich. German women bearing genetically Aryan children would ensure a strong population that conformed to the Nazis ideology of a pure race void of physical or mental impairments. Teens in the Nazi youth movement were encouraged to procreate at very young ages, regardless of marital status. Illegitimate births were welcomed while abortions remained illegal.

However, those rules were meant for German women only. For Jewish women, the rules were very different. In the beginning, women considered *unfit* were encouraged to use contraceptives and resort to extreme measures of abortion as well as sterilization. Many of the women were Jews, Gypsies, and women of conquered areas such as Poland. Although sterilization of men had been around and provided to all men by means of vasectomies or castration, by the 1930s sterilization for women ballooned into more than one hundred different methods. Most surgeons and gynecologists performed a laparotomy, which allowed for fallopian tubes to be either crushed, cut, or removed entirely. Often, the uterus was removed. Later, around 1936, X-rays became a legal method of sterilization, allowing Nazis doctors to experiment with the effects of radiation. Little attention was paid to the sanitary conditions, and as a result, many men and women died from complications and infections.

Between 1933 and 1935, laws were developed, passed, and strictly enforced defining and separating the races as *desirable* or *undesirable*. The Law for the Prevention of Offspring with Hereditary Diseases clearly defined the grounds for eugenic purging and authorized forced abortions were followed by mandatory sterilizations. Drafted by Ernst Rüdin and Arthur Gütt, both psychiatric geneticists, along with lawyer Falk Ruttke, it set a precedent for defining the nine conditions that were assumed to be hereditary. Feeble-mindedness, schizophrenia, manic-depressive disorder, genetic epilepsy, Huntington's chorea, genetic blindness, genetic deafness, severe physical deformity, and chronic alcoholism were the guidelines for abortion and sterilization, and ultimately, extermination.

Many leaders of the German racial hygiene movement jumped on board in great support. As physicians, they began to benefit from the Reich's support for more research and welcomed the funding. However, what motivated most German doctors and psychiatrists to truly champion for the inflicted, the devious and corrupt consequences set forth by the Nazis would lead the medical community down a heinous and despicable dark path. As a result, approximately four hundred thousand German men and women were documented as victims of this mandated sterilization and many because of their *non-Aryan* status.

Jewish women were hiding their pregnancies. As more and more were pushed into the ghettos or herded into concentration and labor camps, pregnancy and childbirth became a sure death sentence. Jewish doctors performed abortions in dark and unsanitary conditions regardless of the advanced stage. As word spread, women were frantically seeking medical help from Jewish physicians and self-made abortionists. Makeshift abortions and deliveries took place quietly and secretly. Pregnancies that had developed to a live birth were delivered in back rooms without medical expertise or equipment and often too early in the stages of pregnancy. Regardless of the outcome for the baby, the mother's stomach would be quickly and tightly bandaged, and she would immediately return to the factory as not to draw attention to her condition.

As the fear spread, less was openly talked about. Bertha needed a plan but wasn't exactly sure how to go about it. And she knew her time was running out. With her small thin frame, she feared she wouldn't be able to hide an expanding waistline for long. And her options were few. With the purging of Jews from media, Bertha was confident her time at the paper was limited. Some of her colleagues at the paper refused to leave and hit the streets harder, distributing any information they could trying to inform the public and gain momentum in the resistance. But it was becoming more and more difficult—and dangerous.

Eventually, for fear of being discovered, Bertha quit showing up to work. No one there would really miss her, as people were being fired daily from the paper. She had little money left and couldn't afford her apartment any longer. Many Jews were forced into small, crowded ghettos with unsanitary conditions and little food. Jewish stores were boycotted as well as all goods and services. All Jewish civil servants were fired, including teachers, doctors, and lawyers.

Bertha started reaching out to friends in hopes of finding a space. She couldn't go back to her aunt Ruth and uncle Boris, not in her condition. To continue a pregnancy there would only draw attention to the whole household. Boris and Ruth were experiencing pressures of their marriage and business. The SS were standing in doorways refusing entry into Jewish businesses. As well, couples married into a Jewish and non-Jewish marriage were being dragged into the streets and ridiculed for their non-Aryan union. As well, she avoided Eddy. Although Eddy was German and accepted as the preferred Aryan race, he was homosexual. Never talked about and hidden fairly well, it was still known in small circles, which made him a target. Keeping a low profile would be a must for him. Bertha was in her first trimester of pregnancy, but feared she would not hide it for much longer.

A few years earlier, while distributing leaflets on the street near Frederick William University, Bertha had met a young biology student named Liselotte Herrmann. She was from a liberal middle-class family, and Bertha was always envious of her ability to attend higher education. However, Liselotte had recently been expelled from the University, along with over a hundred other students, for signing a Call for the Defense of Democratic Rights and Freedoms petition and, as a result, was living with her parents and five other family members. Her stature was small framed with short-cropped hair and round, wire-rimmed glasses, all of which made her appear much younger than her age.

Bertha liked and respected Liselotte as she was incredibly smart, strong, and determined. Bertha always saw Liselotte as a mentor and appreciated her friendship. So when she was invited to move in with the Herrmann family, Bertha was grateful and relieved. The added week or two might be just the time to figure out her next move. And quickly figuring out that move was imperative. Although she now had shelter, Liselotte's family was struggling, too. Food was scarce for everyone. Bertha scavenged for food every day. Quietly and usually in the dark of night, she found small nibbles of food behind the buildings where scraps had been discarded, mostly by Nazi street soldiers.

What little money she had left she kept hidden away in her clothing close to her body, tucked inside her journal. She never went anywhere without both. Liselotte was a source of strength for Bertha. As a comrade of the resistance and a feminist, Liselotte encouraged Bertha to stay strong and focused. Eventually, Bertha confided in Liselotte about Marcus and her pregnancy. She would always remember how kind and nonjudgmental Liselotte had been. Liselotte reminded Bertha of her options. Albeit limited, this helped Bertha to decide her next move.

She began making her plans. At night, she tucked herself into a corner of Liselotte's apartment, away from everyone on the floor between a dresser and a chair. She crouched down onto her only blanket surrounded by five other makeshift beds in the room. She feverishly wrote by a dim sliver of light that pierced a beam through the bedroom door onto the floor by her head. She wrote until her eyelids got heavy and her worry melted away. She wrote of the day, Liselotte, missing good food, and her longing to see her beloved sister, Freida. She no longer wrote of Marcus, and communication between them had stopped. Anonymity had become the norm. Less was written and communicated between people, eliminating paper trails. She never wrote about a baby. It never had a name. And for Bertha, it would never have a place. Eventually, she knew her only plan.

15

Throw your dreams into space like a kite,
and you do not know what it will bring back,
a new life, a new friend, a new love,
a new country
—Anaïs Nin

S HE HANDED HER visa to the ticket agent. Hand trembling, she felt dwarfed by the enormous scale of the Anhalter Bahnhof rail station. Beginning in 1930, steam-hauled express trains spewed and moaned every three minutes from six platforms. At an average of forty-four thousand people daily, the monstrous building was loud and overpowering. With the latest events unfolding, panicked passengers scurried, crowded, and slammed into each other with hopes of ensuring a passage to safety. Some went as far as Palestine, Argentina, Australia, New Zealand, the Netherlands, or Shanghai, China. Many were making their way to France, Austria, Belgium, and other parts of Europe ensuring a quick passage to friends or relatives nearby. For most, however, that would prove to be futile as Hitler eventually occupied many of those areas, and as a result, most were exterminated in the hundreds of camps set up throughout Europe.

In the beginning, emigration from Germany was highly encouraged by the Nazis. The purge of deplorables was the goal. Unless one could secure a place with a sponsor, however, their chances of entering other countries were slim. Many countries feared that some of the more progressive and communist influenced refugees were agitators. As their economy struggled to create and keep jobs for millions, the British were wary of immigrants who could be deemed as competition. But worse, they feared that their impoverished workers may be vulnerable to promises of the communist movement. For some Jews like Marcus, notoriety had its downfall, and the likelihood of escape from Germany was minimal. Bertha knew that her best shot at safety was Great Britain.

Years earlier, Carl and Freida had befriended an elderly woman in their apartment building in London. She was Polish, working as a domestic maid for a wealthy British couple. That connection helped Freida secure a position for Bertha on the outskirts of the city. She was offered room and board with a small pocket of monthly income for her services to clean, cook, and care for an elderly man. The family described Richard as a "sweet, quiet man incapable of caring for himself and was in need of a domestic for his general everyday needs." With a sponsor in place, Bertha was able to quickly shuttle herself to safety. Although grateful for the opportunity, she wasn't excited about abandoning her career in journalism to become someone else's maid. But it was just another part of her changing life she needed to accept.

She boarded the train clutching a small bundle of clothes and her journal. Securely tucked inside her journal were two photographs, one of Freida and the other of her parents on their wedding day. Also, she kept a copy of her first article published in the *Die Rote Fahne.*

She carried only ten Reichsmarks, which, for the time, was the equivalent of about £1.24 or $0.25 in US currency. Anything Jewish owned as well as their personal belongings was deemed by the Nazis as German property.

Many of the Jews being transported to concentration camps were encouraged to bring money, jewelry, and anything else of monetary value under the pretense that new housing and jobs were being arranged for them. Once the Jews arrived at the camps, however, all personal belongs were confiscated and kept by the Nazis. Some Jews relied on creative measures to hide what little personal items they had brought, most of which was jewelry—especially wedding bands. Some were buried, some were tucked in floorboards, and most of were discovered anyway. Many women hid jewelry in the seams of their striped, camp-issued gowns. Unfortunately, all prisoners were stripped of their clothing before being marched naked to the gas chambers leaving jewelry lost forever. There were stories of people swallowing jewels, such as diamonds and other precious gems, only to pass them through their bowel systems later, rinse them off in small containers of soup or water the next day, and repeat the process over and over again until the lucky few were liberated.

But refugees fled with what they could carry on their back. Left behind were titles to homes and businesses, and they were restricted as to how much money they could transfer from German banks. As well, Nazis soldiers stripped them of all jewelry before allowing them to board trains or ships. Jews emigrated from Germany, impoverished and destitute. Hence, the importance of a sponsor was necessary, and most were secured into minimally skilled, low-income jobs.

Before arriving at the station, Bertha had hidden two pieces of jewelry. Her necklace, with the tiny Star of David pendant, had once been her mother's and had been coveted since Bertha's childhood. Although unsure of its monetary value, to Bertha it was priceless. As well, she hid a small delicate watch. Before leaving for Frankfurt, Marcus had slipped a gift box in the top drawer of Bertha's desk at the *Die Rote Fahne*. With an ornate oval face surrounded by tiny diamonds, the watch was secured with a black satin wrist band and a single clasp. There was never a doubt for Bertha of its monetary value. Folded and tucked under the watch was a brief note.

Bertie,

The only real time we have is the present. The memories of our past and the hope of the future are simply gifts. I will forever treasure the gift of you.

Marcus

Bertha converted a children's book to hide her jewelry. The edges of the cover were worn, and the pages yellowed, ensuring its worth to no one. Cutting a shallow square into the lining of the back cover of the book, she placed the jewelry flat into the hole. Then, she carefully glued a decorative piece of paper over the entire back of the inside cover, disguising the makeshift minivault. It was risky, as discovery of her crime would certainly mean confiscation of the jewelry as well as all documentation necessary for travel to safety. And, as always, the potential for arrest and internment loomed as the worst-case scenario.

Waiting to board, Bertha was bombarded with sensory overload. The platform was inundated with the screaming and crying of small children, blasting and gushing of engine steam, exacerbated by the loud inaudible announcements that echoed throughout the station's cavernous chamber—all at once attacking every nerve in her small body. She kept her focus. *Breathe in, breathe out* repeated in her head over and over. Staring at the train and the dark hole at the top of the three steps, she entered the abyss—void of anything familiar.

Her life would be different and not by choice. Gone would be her language, her career, her country, her joy. She dared not project into the future. Her actions and movements had become rote and emotion be damned. She struggled with questions. *Why would so much emphasis be placed on her ancestry as a Jew? With little training and much of the ceremony invented by Freida and herself as little girls simply role playing, why was her very being scrutinized and correlated to a religion she hardly knew?* To uproot a whole country and destroy people over its symbolism was beyond her comprehension. But there she was…joining thousands that held to its value, heritage, importance with the gravity of life itself to devastating consequences.

She squeezed through the car and scrambled for an available space on the long wooden bench. Few made eye contact, and no one smiled. It was a journey of an unknown future. A ticket agent made his way through the narrow aisle, carefully inspecting each right to passage. Close behind were two Nazi police. While most of the passengers kept their heads down and eyes diverted, Bertha's focus was on every detail of that moment. As the police casually strolled behind the ticket agent, their sinister smiles and slight bows of their heads to each passenger ensured their presence was one of complete control. Towering over what appeared to be mostly old men, women, and children, they created a tense and uncomfortable hush. Their uniforms were sharply pressed and garnished with gleaming metals that dangled from colorfully ribboned bars. From each neck hung an iron cross. Its conspicuous polished silver dangled and caught a small flicker of light from the sun beaming in the row of windows of the car.

Blinded in the reflection, Bertha squinted slightly and lowered her head to avoid the contact. Her suspicious movement caught the attention of the two Gestapo. Realizing that he had caused discomfort by his beam of light, he playfully moved his shoulders back and forth, causing the beam to encircle Bertha's face. Humored by his power to control the beam, the two guards laughed out loud and reveled in their taunts. Eventually, they grew bored with the game and moved on.

As well, each guard had a red band worn over the uniform on the left upper arm. On the band was a white circle emblazoned with a black swastika. From Bertha's research at the paper, she knew the symbols and their origins and found it strange how perverse their meaning had become. The Iron Cross, once a military decoration in the Kingdom of Prussia during the nineteenth century and given to Queen Louise as a birthday gift from her husband, King Friedrich Wilhelm III, was typically awarded to military heroes and represented acts of heroism, bravery, and leadership. The Gestapo proudly anchored it at the elite throat of each uniformed policeman. It was no longer earned, but instead confiscated and owned.

The most feared and despised symbol that would forever be recognized as a messenger of hate was the *swastika*. Bertha found this symbol and its transformation the strangest of all. The very word originated almost five thousand years before Adolf Hitler. From the ancient language of India containing scriptures and poems, the word *swastika* means "good fortune" or "well-being." It has, and continues to, adorn temples and other sacred houses of Hinduism, Buddhism, and Jainism. As well, archaeologists have found the *swastika* in Byzantine and Christian art as a symbol of good luck.

Bertha had first discovered the symbol in a book her Uncle Boris had gifted her about America's native people. There, she saw the swastika and its symbolism in a much different form from the Mississippian culture that dated from 1000 AD to 1550 AD. To these ancient peaceful people, the swirling and encircled design represented the sun, the four directions and four seasons. It continues to grace modern pottery, blankets, jewelry, and sand art. However, from his travels in Turkey, German archaeologist Heinrich Schliemann introduced it with German nationalist pride, and it became the symbol of Aryan identity and racial purity, polished with sterilized hate.

Randomly, the guards demanded the passenger's ID. Frightened passengers frantically dug into their jumbled mass of belongings. With purposeful gaze, the guard's eyes stared at the ID, then the passenger, then the ID again—prolonging the agony. Finally, the ID was returned with a swift and startling jet forward. In March, the Dachau camp, located near Munich in southern Germany, had started operation.

Word had spread quickly that prisoners were being transferred there and many by train. For passengers bound for London, the approval of an ID ensured their place in a different direction—one bound to freedom.

A piercing whistle and screeching of metal alerted the pending lurch. They were leaving. Slowly, the train pulled from the station. The car was filled with a deafening hush. Bertha held her breath. Fellow passengers stared at the floorboards of the car. No one looked out the windows. No one waved goodbye. Passengers left standing on the boarding docks were the abandoned ghosts of the escaped few.

Eventually, exhausted passengers settled in to the sound of the rhythmic clicking along the track. One by one, they drifted off to sleep. Bertha's anxiety made it difficult for her to relax. Scanning the car with her eyes, she secretly and quietly reached into her jacket and pulled out her journal. She wrote anything she could remember, and everything she had seen. From an overpowering event or emotion to the smallest detail, she included it all. Nothing was deemed as unimportant.

Although her mind was racing, her body was sinking. She was exhausted. Physically, she continued to endure the aftermath of a horrifyingly brutal procedure. She continued to cramp and bleed. The mere constant washing and changing of makeshift rags was a nagging reminder of great loss, and she worried how she would manage on a train with minimal facilities. She had ended her pregnancy as joylessly as it had begun. It had represented imminent death from its beginning.

Her once heartfelt and mournful melancholy eventually melded into numbness. She could feel her body sinking, sinking into uncontrollable slumber. As her heavy lids challenged her, she quickly secured her journal back into her jacket. She raised her favorite scarf to her chin and cuddled it as she had done many times before. It was a scarf Freida had given to her for her fourteenth birthday. Although washed and worn many times, she could still smell the scent of her sister. It was 1933, and Bertha was leaving Germany, home.

Sinking further, her mind traveled along the tracks. To Freida, Liselotte, Boris, Ruth, Father, Mother. And Marcus.

16

Death ends a life,
not a relationship
—Mitch Albom

TRAVELING THE PICCADILLY lines from Beaconsfield to London was Bertha's favorite moments. She loved the hour-long ride through Colne Valley. Its beautiful mosaic of farmland, woodland, and water stretched two hundred miles with breathtaking views of rivers, canals, and lakes. Summer was approaching, and passing through the lush landscape mesmerized Bertha, allowing her to absorb the majestic scenery. Seldom did she allow her memory to interfere with such tranquility. Five years had passed quickly. She no longer questioned her joy, where it had gone, or if it would ever return. But she was content.

Richard Abbott was a kind, gentle man, and as her employer, he had provided a lovely sanctuary for Bertha. As a long-term editor for the *Observer* newspaper in London, he introduced her to many journalistic connections, which occasionally allowed for small editing jobs. She was grateful for the opportunity and always looked forward to the brief trips. Richard had gained a reputation as one of the most influential editors in London. He was popular for his political articles. Over time, the *Observer* was well known as a quality newspaper with

123

Sunday distribution. His home in Beaconsfield was frequently graced with visitors. Many were journalists. But some were politicians and philanthropists, with an occasional visit from Winston Churchill. As a result, Bertha's popularity grew, and she quickly made friends at the *Observer* and around London.

Richard and Bertha's relationship was one of respect and kindness. Evenings were spent together in the sitting room, reading passages from books and discussing the lives of those who had long passed. Some had dedicated their lives for the common good, while others had chosen a more sinister path. But regardless of the theme, the conversations were exhilarating to Bertha. Richard often encouraged her to share a passage from her journal. At times, he made suggestions for future entries and guided her with bits of his own experiences and recollections. More often, however, he sat quietly and listened. With an occasional nod and grin, he stirred her to continue her thoughts and push through any barriers standing in the way of her dedicated creativity. His display of respect to her and her writing spurred and energized Bertha, and those quiet moments with Richard quickly became her favorites.

She had free access to any room in the house, and there were many. It was a large, two-hundred-year-old farmhouse thick with overstuffed chairs and fringed pillows. Sitting areas were abundant, and each was nestled near a large stone fireplace. Framed photographs were stacked along the mantels and side tables. Although an obvious home of wealth, it was comfortable, humble, and welcoming.

The library was Bertha's favorite room. She loved entering through the large pocket doors into the massive cavern of books that lined the walls from floor to ceiling. Once, when asked how many books were there, Richard laughed out loud and stated that he had lost count after fifteen hundred. He offered the space to her whenever she liked. When finished with chores, she curled up in a large leather chair centered in the library next to the fireplace that beckoned each visitor to its gigantic hearth. With its tall back and ornately carved mahogany arms and legs, the chair made Bertha feel small yet privileged.

There, she would slip off her shoes and slide into one of the back corners. She loved the worn spots of red burnished leather that smelled of cherry tobacco and wondered of the greatness that had graced it over the years. With Frieda's scarf tucked reassuringly under her chin, she spent hours reading and skimming through as many books as she could digest.

Bertha loved Richard's kindness and mentoring, and as a result, she treated him with the utmost of care. Shortly after New Year's Day of 1938, she noticed his movements were slower, and he displayed more difficulty standing. Most recent days were spent in a wheelchair or in his bed. But he never complained, and his voice was soft spoken. Often, he would slip a bit of money into her hand, wink and wave, blessing her on her way to London.

The week had been a flurry of festivities celebrating Richard's ninetieth birthday. The endless parade of visitors, massive amounts of food, and what seemed like the endless chore of clean up exhausted him as well as Bertha and the staff. The train ride to London was a welcomed respite, and Bertha was anxious to arrive at the newspaper. Much had happened, and she needed confirmation from her fellow editors as to the real timeline of events. Although Bertha listened to her radio in her room at night and frequently explored the newspapers that came to the house, she craved the human camaraderie at the paper. She yearned for the company and inspiration of other young professionals.

Until recently, Liselotte had kept Bertha informed through letters. Bertha tucked the correspondence into her journal and savored them for the hour-long ride to London. This ride, however, was void of any letter from her friend. It had been almost a year since Bertha had heard from Liselotte. Shortly after Bertha left for England, Liselotte moved to Stuttgart near her parents and was working as a nanny. In 1934, she gave birth to her son, Walter. The father of the boy, Fritz Rau, had worked as a KPD official and was murdered by the Gestapo that same year. Liselotte and Fritz met as students and fell in love while working through the resistance together. Although deeply saddened by his death, Liselotte expressed great joy with baby Walter. She emphasized the importance of his birth and its relevance as hope through a new generation. As well, she expressed the deepest love and respect for Fritz's dedication as a resistance soldier to what was right and good. Bertha was astounded by Liselotte's wisdom and strength.

Liselotte had also kept Bertha informed of her aunt and uncle. In September of 1935, Nuremberg passed the Blood Protection Law, criminalizing relationships of any form between Jews and non-Jewish Germans. This most certainly included marriage or sexual relationships, which would have endangered Boris and Ruth. Bertha's communication with them was brief and infrequent. Her love and respect for them was endless. But her illegitimate pregnancy and its ultimate termination, as well as her involvement with the communist movement and a socialist newspaper, deterred visits with them. Because of their age, they seemed more like grandparents to Freida and Bertha. Bertha felt protective of them and, therefore, shared her life with them selectively. When Boris and Ruth crossed over into Austria, it was the last time she would ever hear from them again.

As well, Bertha occasionally received brief notes from Marcus. However, in 1935, Marcus and Anna gave birth to a son, Robert, and the only news of them since came from Liselotte. Marcus had never known of Bertha's pregnancy, and she often wondered if it would have made a difference. At thirty-one, she was haunted by twinges of jealousy. The past had left her, just as she had left it.

While in London, she squeezed in as many activities as possible. Before heading for the *Observer*, Bertha checked in at the Bloomsbury

House. It was a haven and resource for immigrants that supported Jewish refugees. Organizations such as the Central British Fund for German Jewry and the Jewish Refugee Committee aided those with housing needs and schools for children. With the perseverance of Director Otto Schiff, Leonard Montefiore, and Neville Laski, such organizations influenced the British government to develop a plan that would allow for the entry of refugees.

Like many other countries, Great Britain was fearful of the economic impact of refugees and remained diligent in containing the influx. Offering aid to the refugees through housing, education, and job training, the volunteer organizations relieved the British government of any financial burden of support. As a result, it allowed for many more refugee entries than had been expected.

Most definitely, Bertha was a beneficiary of such organizations and was grateful to the volunteers and their countless hours of dedicated work. She volunteered and enjoyed her responsibility of meeting with new arrivals and helping them get settled. Knowing their language and a little Yiddish allowed her to ease some of their anxiety and tend to their emotional and psychological needs as well as basic living necessities.

Bertha volunteered with the Society of Friends. In the late 1930s, there were about twenty thousand Quakers living in England. Their organization supported children at Quaker boarding schools and free hostels. Many of the Quakers fostered children, and it was estimated that the Society of Friends was responsible for the safety of over six thousand children. In 1947, American and British Quakers were awarded the Nobel Peace Prize for their generous role in assisting refugees during the Holocaust. Bertha loved their calm, quiet spirit and enjoyed spending time with the children. Sometimes she would read books with them and offer the lighter side of her journal entries. With funds donated by Richard, she often brought journals and pencils to the students and taught them the importance of writing down their thoughts, feelings, and dreams. She knew Liselotte would be pleased that the next generation continued to not only survive but thrive and document the real stories.

Bertha gingerly entered the paper's editing floor, wide eyed and heart racing. Something had happened. The incessant ringing of phones, panicked faces, and the yelling that roared throughout the room sent a chill up her spine. Talk of Great Britain going to war had become the typical topic of discussion. But no one on the train or at the centers where she volunteered had said a word of any such announcement. Bertha knew that, whatever it was, it was huge.

She frantically searched for her new friend, Eddy. Eddy's official job was the mail room. But he aspired to be the next up-and-coming editor, and together, they enjoyed making their way through the chain of command at the *Observer*. Eddy was a tall good looking young man. His blond hair was slicked back tight with a chiseled part that ran perfectly down the middle. The argyle sweater vests with bow ties and baggy, high-waisted pants gave him a boyish look and accentuated his thin physique.

Bertha and Eddy had become fast friends. He was carefree with a wry sense of humor. When budget allowed, they went to the theater together for movies and concerts. Their friendship flourished. However, it remained platonic. There was something about Eddy's movements and mannerisms that caused Bertha to suspect that his preference was of a different gender. But such lifestyles were never talked about or shared. The imminent danger of imprisonment and becoming a social pariah kept many men and women silent. No one was to be trusted with the personal information of one's gender preference. Bertha was indifferent to the sexual preferences of others. Like religion, she struggled with the importance others placed on such matters and chose not to participate in the debates. She loved Eddy, and he was a wonderful friend. That was enough for her. And now, she needed to find him quickly.

The news of Liselotte Herrmann's transfer to Plötzensee Prison in Berlin spread quickly. She was accused of treason. The outpouring for whom all knew her as "Lilo" was overwhelming. Demonstrations spread throughout Europe demanding her release. Eddy and Bertha stayed close to each other. They listened to the reports on the newspaper floor and watched the panic unfold. Along with students Stefan Lovasz, Josef Steidle, and Artur Göritz, Liselotte Herrmann was accused of participating in the Communist Party resistance activities, which included informing friends abroad about National Socialist armament efforts. Obtaining and relaying highly sensitive information about German rearmament, secret weapon's projects, and munitions productions led to their arrest. Production at Dornier aircraft factory in Friedrichshafen and the building of an underground ammunition factory near Celle were listed in the charges as well. The students were said to have relayed all the information to a KPD office in Switzerland.

The news of these student's arrest was shocking to the whole country. Bertha felt weak at the news. Her heart pounded, and she felt as though her knees would fail to support her for much longer. She grabbed Eddy's arm and held tight while listening to the murmurs and gasps across the newsroom floor. The students were symbolic of changing times—a sinister turn. Like many countries all over the world, Germany had had its share of protesting students, typically deemed as idealistic youth stretching the muscles of their naivete. They had always pushed for economic and social change. It was tolerated and expected. To suddenly drag them into the volatile political pool and charge them with dangerous crimes was not expected, however. Germany was arresting its own children.

Eventually, Bertha needed to go back home. Reluctantly, she hugged Eddy and boarded the train. He promised to keep her posted of any changes to Liselotte. But their fears for her were kept silent. If unspoken, perhaps the horrifying reality would just disappear.

The next few months were torturous for everyone. For Bertha, it was unbearable. She barely ate or slept. A constant lump in her throat stifled her ability to chit chat with others and left her perpetually in tears. Many nights, she sat by Richard's bedside and watched him sleep. His monotonous steady breathing was comforting. Yet its juxtaposition with the steady ticking of the large hall clock reminded Bertha of the finality of time. She felt more powerless with every swing of the pendulum. Time was passing, and she was paralyzed with fear. Demonstrations, letters, and pressure from dignitaries worldwide poured into Germany in an attempt to negotiate and save the students.

June 20, 1938, just three days' shy of Lilo's thirtieth birthday, Liselotte Herrmann and her three comrades were executed by guillotine.

17

You cannot find peace by avoiding life
—Virginia Woolf

EDDY INCESSANTLY CALLED the house. But each time, Richard's maid, Lilly, replied the same: Bertha was resting and not taking calls. He left message after message. For weeks, Bertha didn't visit the newspaper, talk on the phone, listen to the radio. She stayed close to Richard and attended to his every need while shutting herself off from the outside world. When needed, she could always be found in the library. She wrote to no one except Freida and continued to write in her journal.

Liselotte's execution had shocked Bertha to her core, as it did around the globe. She could not understand how a world could be so cruel as to take the life of a new mother, a young girl, a smart student. Bertha began to feel extremely vulnerable and fragile. She felt safe in the library. There, no one could find her. However, Richard became deeply concerned about Bertha and continued to encourage her visits to London. For her to isolate herself from the people and activities she loved the most would be devastating to her mood, health, and future.

If Bertha wasn't going to go to the events of the war, it certainly was going to come to her. Although she hesitated to engage in the conversation or attend to any radio announcements, Richard decided that her only salvation was to demand her attention. He knew she loved him and would attend to all his wishes.

Winston Churchill would be addressing a speech to the United States on a live radio broadcast in hopes of gaining military support for all of Europe. Richard instructed Lilly to prepare a pot of his most expensive English tea. It was to be served in his late wife's fine china. The house staff were instructed to bring Bertha's favorite leather chair from the library into his bedroom and place it next to him in front of the radio.

When summoned, Bertha entered Richard's room slowly and cautiously. He had never formally demanded her attention before and she was frightened by the unknown. He instructed her to bring Freida's scarf and take a seat. The tea was poured, and Richard sat silently. No eye contact was made while the soft sound of sipping intertwined with Bedřich Smetana's *The Moldau* quietly playing on the phonograph in the next room.

His choice of music was not by happenstance. Smetana's beautifully hypnotic piece was patriotic poetry. Written in 1874, the melodic story combined a six-movement suite called *Má vlast* (My Country). The listener travels through medieval castles, celestial rural scenes, and legendary tales all set along the Elbe River which ends with the eventual return to victory.

He knew it was one of Bertha's favorite. They had listened to it often and had discussed its importance. She floated through the room with her arms stretched wide in ballet stance, smiling and twirling to the currents of the river. But her greatest joy was the end, marching and saluting to the victory, all the while giggling as Richard smiled and clapped. But this time was different.

This time, as Bertha sat stoically, scarf in lap, eyes fixated on Richard, the music engulfed the room. As the music undulated between visions of woods, fields, and rivers, Bertha sat frozen—her heart pounded. She listened carefully, as always, but this time it was with older wiser ears and a more frightened heart. With each musical transition, her mind was involuntarily pushed through her own horrified visual frames. It ended abruptly, and the silence overwhelmed her. Startled by the clock's chime in the hall, Bertha's hand jerked and splashed tea onto her lap. She quickly grabbed her napkin and dabbed the small droplet stains that invaded her sister's scarf. Richard gently placed his teacup on his bed tray, then reached across the side table and turned on the radio.

On October 16, 1938, Winston Churchill broadcast his words to the world, and it became a speech that would forever be referred to as *The Lights Are Going Out*. The United States had been divided as to its allegiance of support in WWII. Those willing to participate were referred to as *interventionists*. President Franklin D. Roosevelt leaned heavily toward interventionism. However, most American citizens were weary from WWI and the Depression, instead creating an atmosphere of *isolationism*. With the passing of the Neutrality Act of 1937, Congress established legislation prohibiting all trade to nations at war. Unfortunately, this legislation paved the way for Hitler to forcibly obtain land throughout Europe. As well, Japan quickly gained control in the Pacific. The actions helped set the stage for the Great War.

Bertha stared at the radio's small cloth speaker and listened to the crackling frequencies.

It is the future, not the past, that demands our earnest and anxious thought...As we look back over the long story of the nations we must see that, on the contrary, their glory has been founded upon the spirit of resistance to tyranny and injustice...The culminating question to which I have been leading is whether the world as we have known it—the great and hopeful world of before the war, the world of increasing hope and enjoyment for the common man, the

world of honored tradition and expanding science—should
meet this menace by submission or by resistance…We need
the swift gathering of forces to confront not only military but
moral aggression; the resolute and sober acceptance of their
duty by the English-speaking peoples and by all the nations,
great and small, who wish to walk with them. Their faithful
and zealous comradeship would almost between night and
morning clear the path of progress and banish from all our
lives the fear which already darkens the sunlight to hundreds
of millions of men.

Richard reached over and turned off the radio. Bertha softly wept into her scarf. He gently placed his hand on hers and held it firmly. His large palm and crooked fingers surrounded her small, fragile hand. His warmth from holding the tea engulfed her hand and she began to feel the coldness leave her heart. The reassurance of Sir Churchill's speech and the unspoken strength from Richard's hand were, at last, a comforting respite. Words were not needed from Richard. The arrangement of the tea, his dear wife's china, and the accommodation of the chair was loud and clear.

She revealed her tear streaked face from beneath the scarf. With a slight smile, she gazed at Richard through swollen eyes that still managed to twinkle. He winked at her, put his head back on the pillow, and closed his eyes. This was his familiar way of excusing her for the rest of the evening. He had done it so many times before. But this time, it was Richard's confirmation of his confidence in her—his way of letting her go and find her own way. It was a reassuring invitation to embrace the world again.

The commitment of Great Britain and France sent alarms throughout Europe. It didn't take long for chaos to ensue and Hitler's Third Reich to charge. On November 9, 1938, severe violence swept through the streets of Germany. Known as *Kristallnacht* (the "Night of Broken

Glass"), the violence began with thousands of shattered storefront windows of businesses owned and operated by the Jewish communities. They were looted and trashed, along with schools, homes, and even cemeteries. As glass littered the streets, dozens of Jewish people were murdered while others helplessly watched. Hundreds of synagogues were burned to the ground. The next morning, over thirty thousand Jewish men were arrested and sent to concentration camps, leaving mostly women and children placed under strict curfews. With their businesses gone and curfews in place, the already stifling and depressed ghettos swelled into overcrowded and starving cesspools of desperate people.

On November 15, 1938, the press published an announcement by the Minister of Education at the British Embassy in Germany. German-Jewish children would no longer be allowed to go to school with German children. Reports of great abuse and bullying of Jewish children were reported and, as a result, many of the children were kept home.

Eddy's urgent message sent Bertha scrambling for the next train to London. She hadn't been to London since the death of Liselotte. Her emotions were torn between fear of what she would find and the desperate need to be with her best friend. She missed him. A telegram addressed to Bertha Plesser was sent from Martha Wertheimer in Frankfurt. Bertha's fears for Marcus were escalating. Since taking his position at the Frankfurt paper, Marcus had drawn great attention to himself through his activities as well as his reports on the Nazis. Bertha was aware of Martha Wertheimer. As a reporter for the *Offenbacher Zeitung* in Frankfurt, she had written many theater reviews during the Weimar Republic. Bertha admired her work and tried to fashion her own writing after Wertheimer's. But she was also aware that Wertheimer, like many other Jewish journalists, had been fired from her position in the mid-1930s. Bertha was unaware of her life since then and was confused as to why she would be contacting her.

Eddy handed Bertha the envelope. Briefly, she stood in front of him, first staring at the unopened telegraph and then at Eddy. Her eyes appeared to question, as if Eddy could answer. He placed his hand on her shoulder and gave her an encouraging nod. She quickly tore it open and read it out loud. Simply stated, it instructed Bertha to call Martha Wertheimer at the Frankfurt Jewish Congregation office. The closing remark read *URGENT*.

The train ride home felt excruciatingly long as Bertha desperately tried to process all she had been told on the phone by Martha. She knew she would have to tell Richard and feared she wouldn't remember it all. As well, she worried about how Richard would react. Feverishly, she wrote in her journal. Once home, she sat by Richard's bedside with her journal opened on her lap and told him of the call.

After being fired from her position at the *Offenbacher Zeitung*, Wertheimer had been helping operate a soup kitchen for elderly Jews. As well, she had become the Director of the Center of German-Jewish Children at the Frankfurt Jewish Congregation office. She was among many that were working feverishly to aid thousands of Jewish children allowed to leave European countries and travel to England. Known as the *Kindertransport*, Great Britain had agreed to take approximately ten thousand Jewish refugee children. European Jewish parents were scrambling to get their children on trains and ships out of Nazi-occupied areas. Many of the children at the top of the list were of those whose father had already been incarcerated or sent to concentration camps. Fearful of being next on the SS list, mothers were begging the social workers at the centers to include their children on the preferred transport.

Marcus's wife, Anna, was one of them. She had taken her son to the center and pleaded with Wertheimer to include her little boy in the Kindertransport. Marcus had been arrested and, ultimately, sent to Dachau Concentration Camp just outside of Munich. With the capacity to hold approximately five thousand prisoners, Dachau was known as the first concentration camp for political prisoners. Shortly before his arrest, Marcus had instructed his wife to contact

Wertheimer and ensure little Robert a place on the list. Word had spread quickly that children were successfully being transported out of Germany, and their best shot at being accepted in the exchange was proof of sponsor to care for the child. He told Anna that Robert's best chance of acceptance and safe transition to London would be Bertha. He knew Bertha would do this for him. He was confident she wouldn't refuse what was in the best interest of a child. Through connections at the paper in Berlin and his contacts in London, he had tracked Bertha's steps. He knew Wertheimer was the best liaison for getting his son from Germany into Bertha's hands in London.

Within days of Kristallnacht, a delegation of British, Jewish, and Quaker leaders appealed to Prime Minister Neville Chamberlain of the United Kingdom. Previously, the immigration process was slow and tedious, sometimes taking months or years. The plan for Kindertransport was to accept unaccompanied children in groups as opposed to individual applications, hence, speeding up the process. There were strict guidelines, however. The most devastating was the separation of parents from children.

Volunteers worked tirelessly to accommodate those children that were deemed to be in the most urgent of danger. If accepted they would be traveling alone, without their parents. The criteria for traveling children were as follows:

- The children must be seventeen years old and under.
- Small children would be cared for by the older children.
- Personal belongings were a small sealed suitcase with no valuables.
- Monetarily, the child could leave with only ten Reichsmarks or less.
- The children must have a British sponsor who performs as a foster parent and has monetarily secured the agreement with £50.

Ledgers were generated listing children accepted into the program. The specific logs highlighting ports of entrance consisted of four rows of information necessary for a child's entrance: identification number, full name, birth date, and age (in years) at the time of travel. The parents were issued a travel date and details of the child's departure. Children were identified by a tag with twine that hung around the neck and dangled on their chest. On one side was an identification number. On the other side was their name and photo.

Most of the children traveling from Germany, Austria, Czechoslovakia, and Poland traveled to Great Britain by train. Due to restrictions placed by the Nazis, many of the German ports were blocked. Therefore, transported parties first went to the Netherlands and then to the British ports, typically, Harwich, England. From there, children were transported to Liverpool Street Station in London and met by their volunteer foster parents. If foster sponsors were absent upon arrival, hostels, group homes, and farms in England, Scotland, Wales, and Northern Ireland were set up to accommodate those children.

Richard sat silently when Bertha finished speaking and her journal was closed. After a long period of silence, Bertha left the room. Richard's lack of response left her stunned. Deep in thought, he stared at the ceiling, silently contemplating. She waited for his guidance, opinion, help in deciding her fate, little Robert's fate. Confused, Bertha went to her room and sat on the edge of her bed staring at her closed journal. Marcus was in a concentration camp. His wife was frightened and desperate for help. And they were, potentially, starving. The more Bertha visualized the hideous scenario, the worse she felt. She felt sick to her stomach and could hardly catch her increasingly panicked breath. Her focus was interrupted by a soft knock on the door. Slowly, the door opened, and Lilly peeked her head through the narrow crack of the door and frame. Bertha nodded and motioned

Lilly to enter. She entered and handed Bertha an envelope. It was from Richard. Lilly quickly turned and left.

She held the envelope on her lap for a few moments. Finally, she opened it. Inside was £50.

18

There are only two ways to live your life.
One is as though nothing is a miracle,
The other is as though everything is a miracle.
—Albert Einstein

THE HOUSE WAS in constant flurry. The news of a four-year-old little boy from Germany coming to stay had set preparations into swift motion. The staff were gleeful with their chores and couldn't contain their excitement. Bertha wanted to join in, but her fears were staggering. Her consistent obsession with Marcus and Anna's safety disallowed her to embrace joy. As well, she would be responsible for another human being's life, one that is smaller, younger, more fragile than her own. Freida had always taken care of her. Since Freida and her husband moved to London and eventually the United States, Bertha had become accustomed to caring only for herself. Taking care of Richard was easy. He told her of his needs with precise guided instruction. Now, she would care for the immediate needs of another, a little stranger, a child.

And it wasn't just someone else's child. It was Marcus's child. She had managed to push thoughts of her own child deep into the recesses of her memory, so deeply that she had often convinced herself it may not have ever really existed. But the pending arrival of Marcus's son brought feelings to Bertha she hadn't expected. She obsessed of what he might look like, how he will act, and if he would like her. She knew the big picture was to just take care of him, keep him safe, get him past the war, and back to his parents. But her underlying fears for his safety, his parents' survival, and a shaky unknown future nagged at her core.

The termination of a pregnancy severed any potential relationship with her own child as well and created a penetrating guilt that disallowed her to even fathom a connection with another child. Embracing this child, the child of her past lover, the father of her terminated child, was an irony she found too difficult to visualize.

So she threw her energy and focus into lists. She made list after list in her journal in preparation for his arrival. She listed clothes, toiletries, and books. But there was no list that could address the emotional needs—the tools needed for the times when a little boy was scared, sad, or frightened. Bertha had little time. All she could do was concentrate on the concrete needs of food and shelter and just hope the rest would fall into place.

A room was chosen next to Bertha's. It was a beautiful room with a flowered bedspread, crystal lighting, and original art depicting hunting scenes or maidens tending to chores. It was a room any woman would love. When Eddy got wind of this, he booked the first train to Beaconsfield. Richard graciously sent Bertha and Eddy on their way to town for bedroom items better suited for a little boy. They shopped, talked, giggled, and cried. Bertha could not remember a day more joyous. At times, she felt guilty for being so happy. But Eddy was always there to remind her of the greater purpose, the little boy.

Robert was the immediate need. Robert was the focus. As Freida had taken care of Bertha, now Bertha must care for Robert. Freida had been a good teacher and, slowly, Bertha's confidence was beginning to swell. Everything had happened so quickly in the past weeks that she hardly had time to enter all into her journal. Writing Freida would have to wait. She wanted to weigh her words in Freida's letter carefully. Freida's inability to bear children had become the norm; it was barely spoken of anymore. And it certainly had taken a back seat to the world's traumatic events. But Bertha knew Freida and understood she was the older sister, the caretaker. Freida would worry and obsess over the situation. Bertha whispered her secrets to her journal only and spare Freida the pain of what her baby sister had endured in matters of the heart. And news of Robert would be presented as a temporary foster contract, one of emotional detachment for all.

They finished the shopping and headed home with all the goods, excited to make the transformation. Within a couple of days, Robert's room was staged. A simple blue bedspread, embellished with an embroidered nautical compass, masculine lights in the shapes of small barrels, and prints of great sailing ships adorned the walls. Eddy had left a small wooden sailboat on the dresser. He hadn't told anyone of his gift and allowed its presence to speak volumes on its own. Bertha would miss him in the following weeks and would be forever grateful for his friendship and company that weekend.

December 10, 1938, was the day of departure. Running through the streets with parcels and a small suitcase alerted the SS guards standing in doorways. A woman with a small child and luggage, with what appeared to be in a hurried panic, added to the suspicion of Jews in Germany. Anna and her son were detained for over an hour. Consistent questions and careless rummaging through Anna's personal items appeared endless to her. As little Robert stood wide eyed and silent, Anna respectfully and nervously complied with every demand. In the distance, she could hear the bells of the local church ring on the hour. She silently counted each resounding clang, fearful it would ring one too many times. It was a harsh reminder that she was not in control of the events of the day, and depending on how much longer she was detained, it could end quite differently than she hoped. She wasn't sure she could get Robert to the train in time. She wasn't sure if they would arrest her and her child. She was no longer sure of anything.

December 15, 1938, was the day of arrival. Bertha spent several sleepless nights that week. But the night before was excruciating. Random unanswered questions shot in and out of her brain. Her fear was suffocating. She kicked covers off and then pulled them on over and over again in an attempt to regulate her out-of-control inner thermostat. Uncovered she felt open and vulnerable, unprotected. But to be covered felt binding and claustrophobic, stifling every breath.

She periodically rolled and faced a clock with hands that appeared stuck in time. Word had not reached her as to *if* Robert made it to the train. What loomed the largest was fear of him not being there, not getting off that train, and not knowing what happened. Between Berlin and London was a million miles apart. Both children and foster parents would only know their fate in that instant at the station, that instant the train arrived and either connected them forever or filed their abandoned relationships away into the archives faceless names. Over and over, she practiced her greeting. How to greet a small child who had just left his parents was the question she couldn't grasp. Joyous greetings somehow seemed inappropriate and insensitive. And yet, she felt confident that an atmosphere of gloom and despair should be avoided. Her foggy brain and lack of rest was of no help to her. All she could do was get dressed, pack up necessary documents, and be on time at the Liverpool Station in London.

The fostering of children through the Kindertransport was deemed as a temporary situation from the very beginning. Sponsors were categorized in foster contracts, not adoptions. It was understood by all that as soon as the turmoil in Germany settled down, children would be sent back and reunited with their parents. The Kindertransport, therefore, was nothing more than a brief sanctuary, one that shielded the children from the throngs of a violent war and persecution. Thousands of adult Jews had already begun paperwork for their own immigration into England and the United States. Great Britain was confident that, eventually, many of the parents would be reunited with their children in a new home. Unfortunately, extensive waiting periods for travel visas with the eventual closing of German borders inhibited most parents from ever connecting with their children again.

Smiles of anticipation and nervous chatter filled the platform. The buzz of activity was an obvious precursor that a major event or change was about to happen in their lives. Bertha's skin prickled as sounds of chaos invaded her nerves. She tightly squeezed the ends of Freida's scarf. *Breathe in, breathe out.*

In the distance, the train's giant frame groaned and chugged closer. With each turn of the wheel, Bertha's heart kept pace. People cheered and waved. The train came to a slow stop. *What if Robert wasn't on the train?* She tried to dismiss the feeling, but as the intensity of the noise grew, so did her crushing fear. *How would she be able to tell Marcus she had failed him? How could she write to Martha Wertheimer and tell her that Robert never arrived?* There would be no words to express such tragic circumstances of his demise. Now, all she could do was wait. Wait until the hundreds of children poured off the train. Wait until the cheering ceased.

She stood behind the white line with two hundred other people while social workers scurried to greet and direct children as they disembarked the cars. Each child's identification card would be inspected, front and back, and the names and numbers would be carefully correlated with the same on the documented list. As they were processed, a voice boomed over a loudspeaker calling the name of the foster parent responsible for the child. Once introduced, paperwork was signed and exchanged, and the new instant family was formed. Bertha tried to watch as each child was matched with an adult. She wanted to see the different interactions in hopes of gaining helpful clues for her own introduction to Robert. But she couldn't keep her eyes off the train. A girl, boy, chubby blond teen, she inspected each child. The wait was grueling, and she felt suspended in time.

His mother had guided the shy child toward the train. He clung tight to his bear. Anna had instructed him while running through the streets that whatever they dropped would have to be left behind. So he had held tight. Once at the station in Berlin, she quickly hugged him while listing his instructions to write, behave, study hard, all the while reassuring him they would be together again soon. Abruptly, a man in uniform shoved her back behind a yellow line on the floor. A kind lady patted Robert's head, hung a twined cardboard tag around his neck, and swept him up onto the metal steps of the rail car. Once in the car, an older boy lifted Robert up onto a seat so he could see his mother out the window. Many children were smiling and waving out to their parents. Unable to grasp the seriousness and intensity of it all, children acclimated to the idea of a big adventure. They were getting to visit London and had been reassured by parents that it was temporary. Robert was confused. None of the parents would wave back. They all stood silently while uniformed men walked back and forth between them and the train. The SS soldiers instructed the parents not wave or call out. Parents were told that if they broke the rule, their child would immediately be removed from the train, and both would be arrested. But Robert never took his eyes off his mother. And for a moment, he was sure he saw her wink at him.

Bertha spotted the small boy. His knee length breeches and waist-coat were neatly tucked and fitted. He was thin and handsome, with a mass of dark, thick, curly hair and large gentle eyes. She was certain this was Marcus's child. With a small box suitcase in one hand and a toy bear in the another, a social worker reached up and helped him descend the stairs all the while speaking to him in English. He looked confused, frightened, and sad. After processing, Bertha heard her name boom through the platform and sweep through her body and soul. She approached Robert, knelt to his eye level, placed her hand on his, and spoke to him in German. Bertha tried to take his suitcase, but Robert jerked it away. Unwilling to relinquish his possessions, he tucked bear under his arm, carried his bag, and offered his free hand to Bertha.

As they walked through the pandemonium, his eyes jerked nervously through the crowd. He squeezed Bertha's hand tightly. Bertha quickly realized he was overwhelmed and guided him away through the gates onto another platform. Although he could still hear the noise in echoing in the distance, she could see his body and face begin to calm.

Once seated on the train to Beaconsfield, Bertha opened a small satchel. She placed one of her handkerchiefs on his lap and slightly grinned as she realized his skinny legs would not serve well as a tray. She instructed him to put his suitcase on his lap. Then she placed the handkerchief on the case. Once a makeshift table was in place, she handed him the warm tea in a small metal cup. Next, she put two small blueberry scones on the handkerchief. Her slow deliberate movements mesmerized the child. Not uttering a sound, she allowed her actions to speak.

The train was well on its way to Beaconsfield, and Robert had finished his snack. He stared up at Bertha as if for instruction of what to do next. He was pale, with dark circles under his eyes. His exhaustion was obvious. She removed the suitcase and placed it on the floor near his feet. She gently took each dangling foot and placed them on the suitcase for support. Slowly, she pulled Freida's scarf from around her neck and swaddled the toy bear. Robert looked up at her and smiled. Then she put the toy close to Robert's chest and encouraged his arms to snuggle it and keep it close to him. The train gently rocked and clicked through the serene quiet countryside.

Skating through the green pastures and hills, Bertha felt as if the rest of the world was far away. The sleeping child next to her brought her peace and comfort. His light soft breaths rhythmically followed each click of the wheels. As the helpless figure slumped into deep sleep, his arm sprung open from his bear and extended away from his lap, settling on Bertha's knee. Blotchy with dirt, soot, and blueberry stains, she marveled at its small size. His palm was open and appeared sweet and welcoming. She thought to place it back across the bear. Gently, as not to wake him, she cupped her hand around his and kept it there. It was warm and soft. She tilted her head back against the seat, closed her eyes, and drifted off to sleep.

19

We are what we pretend to be,
so, we must be careful about what we pretend to be.
—Kurt Vonnegut

ROBERT LOVED THE small wooden sailboat. Eddy was a frequent visitor, and the sailboat was the center of the day's activities. A picnic in the park was followed by a launch on the shady shallow pond. Eddy secured a long twine to a tiny cleat on the hull, all the while pointing out the specific terminology necessary for each well-trained skipper—windward, starboard, jibe, etc. Robert listened intently, his eyes bouncing back and forth from Eddy's voice to the boat. Over time, Robert absorbed English and was able to easily interchange between it and his native language of German. Bertha had enrolled Robert into the village English school immediately when he arrived. Although he remained quiet and withdrawn, he quickly adapted to the schedule of the day and appeared content with his activities. It was apparent he preferred to be alone, and he spoke only when responding to questions. Initiated conversation was reserved for his bear, and it was always in German. Bertha was careful to encourage the retention of his German language. She feared he would forget quickly and suffer the consequences when returning home to his parents.

Richard enjoyed having a child in the house. When his health allowed, Bertha wheeled Richard into the study where he could watch the little boy play with puzzles, games, or study geography with her. He quietly watched and smiled as he reveled in the young boy's intelligence. Robert's favorite activity with Richard was reading and Richard was grateful for the company. Before bedtime, Bertha instructed Robert to scrub his face and hands clean, brush his teeth, and choose a book off the shelf for reading time. She even made a matching nightshirt for his bear. Together, they entered Richard's room and sat by his bedside. While Robert read his book aloud, Richard and Bertha quietly sipped their evening tea and listened. After reading, Richard reached over and patted the boy's hand and complimented him on a fine job.

Bertha discovered a small wrinkled photograph of Robert's parents tucked in his suitcase. Marcus and Anna were heavily clad in coats, hats, and gloves in a snowy Frankfurt park with little Robert toddling near their feet. They looked happy and content and remarkably handsome together. Within a day, Bertha secured the photograph in a small silver frame with ornately carved sweet cherubs and placed it on his nightstand next to his sailboat. Each night, Bertha instructed him to wish his parents a *gute nacht* (good night). She frequently mentioned them in regular conversation, referring to them as *Vater* (father) and *Mama* (momma).

Shortly after Robert had safely arrived to England, Bertha received a telegram from Wertheimer that Anna had been arrested in Frankfurt. According to the wire, it was believed that Anna had been taken to Ravensbrück, a concentration camp reserved for women. Located in northern Germany, it was known as one of the largest camps, imprisoning over ninety thousand women including Polish, Jewish, Russian, French, and Dutch. In the beginning, most of the women were slave labor for factories owned and operated by Siemens Halske, an electrical engineering firm that later developed the secret individual cipher systems allowing Germans to pinpoint enemy locations through codes. Later, those codes would be broken by Sweden and Great Britain and ultimately aided in the Nazis demise. However, before that could happen, many of the women succumbed to medical experiments that tested the effectiveness of sulfonamides.

Often, wounded German soldiers suffered from infection, gangrene, and tetanus. German doctors were experimenting on camp prisoners to try and find a remedy for the infection through synthetic agents. After creating wounds on prisoners, surgeons would tie off blood vessels that supplied the wound with necessary circulation to ward off infection. Once infected, the Nazi camp physicians would aggravate the wound by forcing wood shavings and ground glass into the wound before applying the drug to determine the effectiveness. Years before, this drug had already been tested on animals, medically researched, and documented in the medical community as inappropriate and unsuccessful. As with most experiments performed on millions of prisoners throughout European Nazi camps, prisoners either died from the experiment or became permanently disabled. Regardless, almost all of them were exterminated afterward.

Once tucked in, Bertha sat on the edge of the bed and gently stroked his hair. The large soft curls appeared to have a mind of their own and she quietly smiled and enjoyed the fact that they could not be controlled. Although careful to allow Robert his space and feelings, she was pleasantly surprised when the little boy initiated the physical attention he needed. It was apparent that he felt safe with Bertha and, therefore, didn't hesitate to reach out.

Each night, he rolled to his side and faced Bertha, curled up into a small tight ball, and snuggled close to her. The only thing between them was Bear. With each soothing stroke to his hair, he fell deeper into sleep. She found herself in love with the little boy that had been dropped into her world. Initially, she had tried to resist the temptation of developing too many feelings for him, as she knew it would be short term. She desperately tried to contain her feelings and remembered her place in the scheme of things. A nanny, a nurse, a mentor—those were her titles, and she needed to remember that.

But like her love for Marcus, she couldn't control the true feelings of her heart. She loved Robert and worried about what the future may demand. Richard suggested that Robert address her as *Aunt Bertha*. He encouraged her to act as extended family and not as a foster parent, confident that Robert would feel closer and more secure if he felt love from family instead of strangers. So Bertha often stated to Robert that he had both English and German family. She even shared photographs of Freida and Carl and incorporated the United States in their geography lessons. Although she had no intentions of taking him there, he displayed great interest in America and appeared to crave books of its history. His favorite was of the Old West, and he had told Richard that, someday, he would like to live on a ranch and be a cowboy. Too young to question the lineage, Robert easily accepted his extended family.

Time passed quickly, and although the war continued, day after day of regular routine and full schedule kept everyone busy and preoccupied. It was 1940, and Robert had just celebrated his sixth birthday. Excited over his new collection of toys and books, he quickly chose his favorite book. Zane Grey's *Riders of the Purple Sage* became the preferred reading at night. Still early in the evening, Bertha timed the ritual carefully to give Richard and her their peace at the radio alone. She shielded the little boy from the radio newscasts to protect him from the horror and rumors of the war, specifically of any news of labor camps.

Bertha couldn't help but be preoccupied with thoughts of Marcus and Anna. Knowing that they were both incarcerated, she became increasingly worried about Robert's future. Richard became concerned, as well, and began expressing his concerns to Bertha. He suggested she consider going to America with Robert and staying with Freida and Carl, *just for a while*. Bertha was torn in so many directions with such a suggestion. She found it incomprehensible to leave Richard in such a fragile state. She knew deep in her heart that if she left him she would never see him again. Once in America, it would be impossible for her to travel back to England during the war. As well, she couldn't fathom taking Robert away from his parents. When the war ended, and they were released from the camps, it would be easier to travel by train if still in Europe. Most European civilians were unaware of the magnitude of deaths that were taking place in the camps, and therefore, were hopeful to be reunited with family once the war ended.

After a couple of years, Great Britain's Royal Air Force developed superb success. That success infuriated Hitler. Out of retribution, he pledged to obliterate Great Britain's London center. In September of 1940, bombings of London started. Regular bomb raids were practiced and ultimately performed there. Germany declared the raids as Blitzkrieg (Lightning War) that specifically targeted industry in towns and cities. For eighteen months London was relentlessly besieged with air raids by the Luftwaffe. When the barrage of firepower ended, over forty thousand civilians had lost their lives. Homes were destroyed, and the damage was estimated at a loss of more than a million houses.

Bertha had stopped going to the paper and was careful about taking Robert on excursions too far from home. She lived in constant fear that the Nazis would make their way to England and encamp her and Robert. However, when the bombings ended in London, everyone seemed to breathe a little easier. Bertha stayed in constant communication with Eddy. She was continuously worried about him, but he refused to leave London. He had secured his rightful place at the paper, adding more editing and writing assignments to his belt, refusing to vacate what he saw as his well-deserved space. The war kept all media in a constant flurry, and he couldn't fathom leaving such momentum.

At the same time of the Blitzkrieg on Great Britain, a Tripartite Pact was formed between Germany, Italy, and Japan. It became known as the Axis Alliance. Presiding over territories in Europe, North Africa, and East Asia, they partnered their common interests of territorial expansion as well as the attempt to destroy Soviet Communism. Initiated conflicts by the three powers globally intensified World War II. With Japan's invasion of southern Indochina, Franklin D. Roosevelt ordered all Japanese assets frozen. America was hopeful that, with economic sanctions and embargoes, Japan would be hindered from expanding further, especially into the West Indies. As a result, Japan's navy and air force attacked the United States on December 7, 1941 in Pearl Harbor, Hawaii.

Alternating declarations ensued. December 8, the United States declared war on Japan; December 11, Germany and Italy declared war on the United States; and finally, the United States declared war on Germany and Italy. Support for isolationism in the United States eventually faded, and more than two years after the start of World War II, the United States had finally entered the conflict.

Although the news of America's involvement in the war against Germany and Italy was a huge relief to the people of Europe, the years of war were taking its toll. By 1942, millions of young men had perished while serving. And millions more were civilians. Listening to the news was frightening and exhausting. Eddy was finding it difficult to take time away from the newspaper and his visits were greatly reduced. Richard was sleeping more and more. Although Bertha continued their evening ritual of tea and radio at his bedside, typically she sipped her tea and listened while Richard slipped in and out of deep slumber. At ninety-four, his body was failing him, and Bertha saw the spirit begin to fade as well.

Years had passed without any news of Robert's parents. Their little boy would be turning eight in the coming year, and Bertha couldn't help but wonder what it was like for them not knowing about their own child. She continued to speak about Marcus and Anna as small reminders to Robert. But time was taking its toll with his memory as well. Bertha was starting to realize that Marcus and Anna were quickly becoming a small photograph of strangers to the child, and Bertha's attempt to preserve them in his memory was fading. She could tell him brief stories about his father's personality and talents when working with him at the paper in Berlin. She often praised his notoriety as a fine journalist. But, of course, her personal memory of him was kept locked in her heart and journal, and she noticed Robert tiring of the same stories over and over of a man he barely remembered.

For memory and stories of Anna, Bertha was at a loss. She had never met her, and Marcus had shared very little of the woman he would eventually marry. Therefore, she kept mention of Anna's name with stories of future possibilities. She reminded Robert of "how surprised Mama will be to see you getting so tall." Or, perhaps, "how she will giggle when she sees bear's nightshirt." But Robert rarely responded. Usually, he would just shrug his shoulders with an air of indifference.

His silence was confusing to her. His lack of memory came across as polite indifference, and Bertha found it disturbing. She didn't remember her own parents. Her only memory was a prefabrication of Freida's doing. But Bertha was aware at a very young age that the stories Freida shared were just that to Bertha—stories. She, too, preserved what little memory she could in a single photo. And it was possible that she and Robert would always share that dark common corner of their childhood. Her biggest fear was that Robert's reactions were of profound sadness. Her guilt of consistently reminding him of parents he may never see again began to eat at her very soul. Her confidence in the future for Robert was changing with each passing birthday. He was outgrowing bear, and they no longer slept in the same bed together. It was clear that bear was still important to Robert, but just not embraced in the same way any longer. Bear stayed on a little chair next to Robert's bed, another item that Robert had outgrown.

After a long, grueling wait, Bertha received a letter from Freida. During the Blitzkrieg, all mail had halted. It was a joyful respite when hearing from her sister. Their exchanges were kept selfish from the war and held firm to sharing only simple everyday occurrences. They relished in their sisterhood.

However, Freida's news of Carl's enlistment into the United States Navy was a shock to Bertha. She found his decision to enlist overwhelming and disturbing. Periodically, Carl had stressed his anger and sadness for his native country. Although grateful to be in America, he suffered guilt from not being able to participate in helping win back the country he knew and loved. His parents and younger sister had not communicated in months, and the last letter he had received from his sister expressed deep concern over the intense atmosphere. In the mid-1930s, his family sought refuge in Norway. It was a safe haven for refugee German Jews until Germany's invasion April 8, 1940. When a collaborationist government led by the fascist party leader Vidkun Quisling muscled its way into Oslo, King Haakon VII abdicated as prime minister, refusing to cooperate with invading Nazis. Ultimately, the Norwegian king and other ministers of his cabinet sought refuge, and that finally led them to the United Kingdom.

By 1942, most Norwegian and German Jews were deported from Norway, shipped to Germany, and exterminated in Auschwitz-Birkenau, one of the largest established killing centers. Unaware of his family's fate, he felt frustrated, fearful, and helpless. His enlistment was his only immediate emotional recourse.

Bertha was proud of Carl and grateful for the sacrifice he was willing to endure. She feared for his safety, of course. But her immediate response was the emphatic protection and concern for her sister. Freida's inability to bear a child and the long separation from her sister was worrisome enough for Freida's emotional health. With the addition of Carl's enlistment into the Navy, Bertha feared that Freida's anguish would be too much for her to withstand.

Both Carl and Freida had been able to avoid the few German and Italian internment camps run by the US Department of Justice. Once committed to the war, the United States detained approximately eleven thousand ethnic Germans in internment camps under the Alien and Sedition Acts. Most of the German and Italian residents had already become US citizens, and they were numbered in the millions. Unlike Japanese citizens, the German and Italian citizens had acclimated and blended into American society easier, leaving the smaller population of Japanese citizens suspect after the attack on Pearl Harbor. German and Italian citizens who were suspect and, therefore, incarcerated into the internment camps were typically coastal residents, and many had moved farther inland.

Now, Carl had taken the personal and patriotic leap into the US Navy. For Jewish men fighting in a war where the persecution of Jews was the focus, save whatever his citizenship may be, certainly placed them in a dangerous and precarious arena. For any serviceman, the looming fear of capture was consistently on their minds. Hence, once enlisted, all servicemen received the added necessary training for procedures related to becoming a potential prisoner of war.

Over 550,000 Jewish men and women served in the US armed forces during World War II. Along with other service men, Jewish soldiers wore the mandatory *dog tags*, or identification tags. Between 1941 and 1952, all tags contained personal information (i.e. name, serial/service number, date of most recent tetanus shots, and blood type). Each service member wore the two small metal plates on a chain or cotton rope around their necks. The tags were a way for medics to help the wounded as well as identifying the dead. During WWII, an added feature was incorporated—a single letter describing the religious affiliation of the serviceman. The purpose was to ensure that the wearer's religious needs were properly met—P (Protestant), C (Catholic), and H (Hebrew). The absence of a letter indicated that there was no religious preference.

The single letter of H could have meant the difference between life and death for a Jewish serviceman fighting in Europe or the Soviet Union. And, although POW's were protected under the Geneva Convention, the ultimate decision could easily become the decision of the labor camp's commander at the time. Soviet prisoners fared worse, and they were typically treated as Jews subjected to hard labor, starvation, and extermination. Some Jewish servicemen chose the absence of the letter completely. Some chose the letter H but, in a panic, chiseled it off the small plate once on enemy lines. But for many, the absence of their Hebrew identification was a disservice to their heritage and family.

Carl was being sent to the South Pacific as part of his naval service. Whatever he chose to do on his tags would be less scrutinized by the Japanese. Bertha and Freida were unaware of letters on tags, and Carl never discussed it with them. What he chose to do would be safely tucked away in a wooden box with other memorabilia, photos of him in uniform, and small trinkets of Carl's deceased family that Freida saved until her death.

Freida's letter continued, as if her news of Carl was just another added daily event in her life. Bertha knew her sister well. Freida was one to "march on and be a brave little soldier." She chose to write of the beautiful seasons and what inventive recipes she had developed since rationing had started in the United States. For Bertha, it was an indication of Freida's strength. Years later, Bertha's journal revealed her discovery that it was actually Freida's way of helping Bertha cope and stay strong. She was elated to hear about Freida's gardens and recipes, as Great Britain was rationing as well.

Richard's entire household embraced and shared in the responsibility of providing adequate food for the household. Growing their own vegetables, raising their own livestock, and utilizing every square inch of land for agriculture provided a communal sense of awareness. Those unable to join the military felt involved in the effort and fight for the war by growing their own food. Not only did it strengthen the economy at home it provided extras for the young men and women fighting abroad. Amazingly, reports of general health improvements among civilians started circulating. Sugar was also rationed, requiring inventive measures for something sweet. Often, carrots were used as a replacement for sugar. Children were frequently seen enjoying carrots on sticks known as *lollies*.

With their own fresh foods, medicinal herbs, and the added exercise, both Great Britain and the United States began to reap the added health benefits of what they referred to as "victory gardens." Freida even bragged about Eleanor Roosevelt's garden at the White House. As always, her letter ended with a gentle sigh. She missed Bertha and wished she could see her soon. She always managed to squeeze in an offer on the last line…her home was welcome to her little sister and precious Robert—anytime.

Bertha was confident that Freida's letter was her way of trying to display great bravery while she nervously occupied her time with Carl's absence. Carl's safety moved to the top of the priority list for both sisters and, with each passing day, the grueling wait for any news of him consumed all thoughts.

Sitting on the side of her bed, Bertha held the letter close to her heart for a long time. Freida had been the only family she had ever really known and her love for her sister remained strong. But she was dedicating her love and responsibility to Richard and Robert and felt the move would be too devastating for all. She neatly folded the letter back into the envelope for safekeeping and tied it to the others secured by a ribbon. She kept them in a small wooden box next to her bed. When waiting for the next letter became too unbearable, she untied her private stash and read them all again.

The next day, while Robert was in school, Bertha sat by Richard's bedside and listened to her favorite radio program. *In Your Garden* was hosted by a gentleman named C. H. Middleton and was listened to by millions of people in Great Britain. His listeners enjoyed advice on growing, cooking, planting, and overall healthy food choices and recipes. Bertha couldn't help but smile and think of how Freida would enjoy such a program.

She sat quietly listening and sewing. Robert's knickers were becoming worn and would soon be too small. As little boys could do, he had managed to put holes in both knees as well as in the pockets. But repairing the small holes might extend the life of the fabric just a little while longer until they could be replaced with a more appropriate size. She paused and watched Richard sleep. He was rarely awake, and he struggled to breathe. She visualized stitching a small hole in his heart and, like Robert's knickers, extending Richard's life just a little longer.

Throughout the years, visitors had become few and seldom, and the letters from distant relatives had ceased long before. Occasionally, Richard's longtime friend and physician made brief house calls to check on him and chat. But he was getting older too, and his own health made the arduous trip impossible. It had become obvious by his lack of recent visits that there just wasn't much more he felt he could do for Richard. So she sat by his side, listening and stitching, as she had done for almost a decade.

Although she had dreamed of her life back in Germany, an apartment in London, working on the paper, her first trip to the United States, seeing her sister again, all the dreams that serve as small windows to a young woman's future plans—she wasn't ready. She wasn't ready to move Robert from little boy breeches to long pants. Pants that would carry him to independence. And she wasn't ready to move on with her life without Richard. She wasn't ready to say goodbye to any of that, or to him. Maybe just one more stitch, one more radio show, one more breath.

20

The things you do for yourself are gone when you are gone,
but the things you do for others remain as your legacy.
—Kalu Ndukwe Kalu

S
HE SAT SILENTLY and motionless. The office was dark, dusty,
and claustrophobic. It took her eyes a while to adjust from bright
to dark. Spring was finally blooming outside, and the sun was
a welcomed respite from the long, difficult, and depressing winter.

A secretary led Bertha through the door, politely motioned her
to sit in a chair, and offered her tea. When Bertha declined, the
secretary swiftly left the office closing the door behind her leaving
Bertha alone to sit and wait in the gloom of a room shut off from the
outside. Dirty windows exacerbated the inability for the sun to shed
any light. She occupied her thoughts with the contents of the room.
Papers were everywhere, and they were stacked high above her head.
The desk was cluttered with books, a dirty ashtray, and three tea cups,
abandoned with dried, encrusted leaves. Books were jammed tight
onto the shelves, stacked on chairs, and strewn across the floor, all of
which were labeled with complex and confusing titles.

As executor to the will, she was nervous thinking she may be
responsible for some of that knowledge. She knew nothing about
wills or estates or the laws attached. Since Richard's death, she had

been bombarded with phone calls, telegraphs, and paperwork that she clearly didn't understand but signed anyway. She found it shocking that Richard would leave her with such a responsibility. Although willing to take care of him in death as well as in life, she was confident he could have found a friend, relative, business acquaintance, or anyone with more savvy of such matters.

The past two weeks had been a blur. She had been so inundated with the funeral arrangements that she hardly had the time for thoughts of where and how she and Robert would continue their lives. Upon Richard's death, she'd received a letter from his lawyer informing her of her duties as executor of his will. Outlined in great detail were instructions for his funeral, announcements, and all other arrangements necessary for his transition from house to grave. She assumed she had been summoned to the lawyer's office to be handed her final and official notice of termination.

Of course, Richard's death was the death of her job. She was surprised, as she had expected final notification in a letter like any other job. Instead, she was to appear in person. She was hopeful that the notice would give her some time to make necessary housing arrangements elsewhere. When taking the job with Richard, Bertha hadn't planned on staying long—just long enough to get through the war, get herself back to the paper in Berlin, and eventually get Robert back to his parents. Her added feelings of love and devotion to Richard hadn't been planned either. Nor had she planned on being there for his death. Unemployed, homeless, and surrogate motherhood had never entered her mind. On top of it all, mourning the loss of a dear friend was excruciatingly painful. He was no longer just her employer. He had become family. And she realized he was the first loss in her life that she actually watched buried.

Despite the dingy atmosphere of the office, Bertha appreciated the moment of quiet solitude. She hadn't had such a moment in months. As her eyes scanned the room, noting each careless and random pile, she couldn't help but smile to herself. For a moment, she thought of how she would describe that office to Richard and the great laugh they would share later. Her heart slightly sank with her faded illusion. The fireside chats in the library, bedside tea at the radio, and their sharing of little Robert's accomplishments were forever gone. Although she had cried herself to sleep every night, eventually, she no longer had the tears.

She turned her thoughts to the sweet times they had spent together and their mutual love for Robert. He was like a grandfather and mentor to them both. Robert had remained quiet, choosing to spend solitary time in his room with books. When passing Richard's room on the way down the hall, she noticed Robert simply ducked his head to pass quickly. She worried about him but struggled to find soothing words that might help. Eventually, small evening rituals were invented to replace the times with Richard. Reading by the fire in the library curled up together in the leather chair was the perfect way to end the day.

Often, after school, Robert could be found in the kitchen working on a large jigsaw puzzle chatting with Lilly while she prepared dinner. Lilly was young and energetic, and Bertha understood why Robert liked her. She was closer in age to him than anyone else in the house, and she treated him more like she was a big sister than just the housemaid. Although she could tell Robert was sad and missed Richard, he appeared to handle it all very well, and Bertha was amazed at his strength. And yet, perhaps it was an indication that watching the natural progression of age and dying was, indeed, easier than people just disappearing in your life, never to be seen or heard of again. One had closure; the other didn't.

She knew their days together were quickly fading when, one spontaneous evening Richard had asked her to turn the radio off and read to him. He requested Lord Byron's *The Tear*. Richard quoted Lord Byron often. She loved their discussions of Bryon, his exotic travels, excessive debts, and scandalous affairs, all the while struggling with the disability of a clubbed foot was enticing to Bertha. Byron was the perfect example of the tortured, brilliant poet. Although they had read many of Bryon's works together, they had not yet explored "The Tear." Softly, she read the unfamiliar prose. It was captivating and melancholy.

Ye friends of my heart,
Ere from you I depart,
This hope to my breast is most near
If again we shall meet,
In this rural retreat,
May we meet, as we part, with a Tear.

When my soul wings her flight
To the regions of night,
And my corpse shall recline on its bier;
As ye pass by the tomb,
Where my ashes consume,
Oh! moisten their dust with a Tear.

When finished reading, Bertha placed a velvet ribbon on that page to secure its place forever. Holding the book close to her heart, she sat and watched Richard sleep. For what seemed like an eternity, she stared at his face and hands. She marveled at his skin. At ninety-four, it was remarkably smooth and clear—youthful beyond his years. She memorized the walls of photographs and paintings, and his bedside table. She wanted to remember every detail of the room, down to the smallest of trinkets that were essential for the importance of the day. The pills, teacup, radio, handkerchief, comb, nail clippers, Bible, small photo of his wife, a few cards from friends, some unopened.

Richard had been stripped of all personal dress that had been so very important in his life. No longer did he dress for the day in tapered wool slacks with a sharp crease, starched shirt, and tweed jacket. His thick white hair was slicked back framing his chiseled face and steel-gray eyes. He was a stunningly handsome man and viewed much younger than his age. Regardless of lack of excursions or visitors, Richard's impeccable appearance was dignified and proud. For the remaining months of his life, however, such adornments had waned. His blue-plaid pajamas and favorite chenille blanket had become the only necessary wear. His wedding ring, which he never removed from his finger, remained as the only reminder of his past.

Bertha had written in her journal that night. Her experience with Richard's death was a stark contrast to those she had lost before. For her, the loss of loved ones came from messages, telegrams, posted bulletins on synagogue doors, or newspapers. She thought of her father and of Liselotte. People dragged off to guillotines, concentration camps, war—they left with no reminders of who they were or of where they had originated. Bedside tables sat silently in abandoned rooms where surfaces were void of photos, wedding rings, or cards.

Watching Richard die was sad and, yet, peaceful. His passing was different. She was grateful she was there and could comfort him. She placed every detail of that night into a visceral photograph that would forever remain deep into the safe corners of her heart.

Eddy attended the funeral and spent a few days afterward to bring a little light back into their lives. He was his usual charming self, consoling her all the while entertaining Robert. Robert had grown fond of him and always looked forward to his visits. For the young boy, Richard's passing was just another separation in his life. He didn't speak of it, showed quiet and minimal remorse, and silently distanced himself from most of the activity that surrounded him. Thankfully, Eddy proved there was still a bit of joy in Robert's eyes, and this greatly relieved Bertha.

Leaving the lawyer's office, Bertha felt relief and awe. He listed each detail of the will and she was astounded at how organized he could be in such a chaotic room. Richard had been specific as to where, whom, and how the bulk of his total estate's worth would be distributed. His belongings, including home, land, and contents, were to be sold in an estate sale. Once sold, the monetary distribution would begin. For Lilly and the rest of the house staff, each would receive a monetary bundle, small compared to Richard's wealth, yet largely generous to the recipients. Bertha was confident that their inheritance would greatly improve their lives, and she was excited to share the news with each of them. As well, Richard had arranged for a few donations, including the Central British Fund for World Jewish Relief and the Society of Friends, the Quaker group with which Bertha had volunteered.

Small trinkets were mentioned to be sent to dear friends, mostly in the form of photographs and books. A special page was designated to Bertha. The lawyer had been careful to read each detail and confirm her understanding along the way. After reading the decree, he looked deep into Bertha's eyes as he explained the special instructions of Richard's wishes.

Bertha stared back. She nodded but remained speechless. He handed her the packet of paper. She thanked him and left the office. Richard had left the bulk of his estate with Bertha. As well as a large monetary gift to her, a hefty trust fund had been established for Robert's education. Richard stated that Bertha could keep the library leather chair and any book of her choosing. But his instructions were clear and exact: using her inheritance, she was to take Robert to America and stay there until after the war. He listed journalistic contacts in New York and New Jersey who would aid in finding her work. He instructed her to contact them upon her arrival. As well, he used his influence to ensure the appropriate paperwork necessary for their safe and legal travel out of Europe.

Before getting on the train home, Bertha stopped at the London paper to see Eddy. They tucked themselves into a corner of a café patio near the station. In the warm sun, they talked freely and privately. As she told Eddy of the inheritance and Richard's appeal that accompanied it, she confided in Eddy that she hadn't planned to move to America. The questions flew from Bertha's mouth to Eddy's ears.

How would she take Robert away from his home and parents? Where would she work in America? How could she leave Eddy, her dearest friend? The more she talked and questioned it all, the more it seemed impossible. The fear of it swelled. She struggled to catch her breath. Every negative scenario she could think of spewed from her mouth at lightning speed.

Eddy sat patiently, allowing her to vent and release all the fear. She talked and talked until she finally buried her head into his shoulder and sobbed. Her sorrow wasn't because of Richard's demand. She was overwhelmed at his generosity. She hadn't cried in weeks, and she was exhausted. She was so very grateful, and yet, so very confused.

Eddy was the perpetual good friend, listening, nodding, holding hands. His list of opportunities was simple. He reminded her that her home would be wherever she and Robert would be, she could work for a New York paper, and they would be safer and happier there with Freida. Bertha couldn't resist a slight smile when Eddy reminded her that the greatest benefit of living in America was the visits from British friends.

Knowing how much Bertha loved Robert, Eddy felt it was a good time to tell her of the latest development concerning Martha Wertheimer. Because of Martha's notoriety, a wire had been sent to all the newspapers of the latest disturbing news of Martha. Sensitive to Richard's recent passing, Eddy chose to wait until he could talk to Bertha face-to-face of Martha's fate and the potential meaning of it all for little Robert and his family.

On June 10, 1942, the Gestapo arrested over fifteen hundred Jews from Frankfurt and the surrounding areas to transport them to the death camps in the east. Wertheimer had continued her work with the Jewish Community Fund and was targeted by the Nazis. To set an example of public display, they arrested her and ordered her to take charge of organizing the group, forcing her to march members of her own community to their ultimate deaths. Along with the fifteen hundred others that day, Martha Wertheimer was never heard from again.

Eddy reminded Bertha that all communication between Martha and Robert's parents had stopped long ago. Martha's disappearance was not a good sign for Robert's future in Germany. Although not confirmed, exterminations in the death camps had quickly moved from rumor to actuality. Years had passed, and so far, no word of any of the ten thousand Kindertransport children had been reunited with their parents. If Robert were to end up one of the lucky one percent, his parents would eventually be released and reunited with their child.

But as time had passed, the probability of this grew slim. And if the war took a turn in England, both Bertha and Robert would be in grave danger. Again, he reminded Bertha that a move to America could be just temporary and, when all is well with the world again, she and Robert could return. He planted the seed of the joy Freida would feel spending time with her baby sister. Still childless and Carl away at war, Freida had been suffering from deep melancholy and desperately needed her sister. As well, Robert could benefit from a male figure when Carl returned home.

Eddy encouraged Bertha to think of it as a great adventure, an education for both her and Robert, and just another path in life that twists and turns to better places. He reminded her of how brave little Robert was when his train swept him away from his parents and, now, Bertha must show Robert her courage as well. She must help him to grow as a survivor.

In an exuberant show of joy and encouragement, he raised his arms high into the air, threw his head back, and in wild abandonment exclaimed into the heavens, "You're going to America!"

21

That it will never come again
is what makes life so sweet
—Emily Dickinson

ROBERT WAS TEN years old when WWII ended in 1945. As the years passed, the little boy had quietly grown accustomed to the typical lifestyle of any American-born child. School, baseball, camping, and summers at the lake was his life. Anything else was simply a faded memory locked in the evolutionary journey of his past. Like many young children of the Kindertransport, Robert barely remembered his parents, Germany, or his native language. And like most of the children, his connection to any of it was severed by the death of his parents.

Robert was one of millions globally impacted by the war. From September 1, 1939, through September 2, 1945, it is estimated that approximately sixty million military and civilian lives perished in the 2,194 days of brutal conflict. Approximately six million of them were concentration camp executions. Of the ten thousand children removed from Germany in the Kindertransport, most never saw their parents again. Older children were often placed into the labor force of either factory or farm. Many enlisted into the army as soon as they were of age. Unfortunately, mistreatment, abuse, and anti-Semitism plagued others.

But for the lucky children, the ones placed in loving homes, the guilt, shame, confusion, abandonment, and great loss followed them throughout the rest of their lives. Although grateful to both birth and foster parents for the life given, often the separation was too difficult to absorb. As a result, many children simply fell silent of their past. What little Robert could remember, he kept to himself.

News of Marcus's death spread quickly throughout Germany due to his notoriety and connection to Rabbi Leo Baeck. Baeck had refused to leave Germany. He was committed to helping others in their attempt to escape and represented those incarcerated. Unfortunately, Rabbi Baeck, by word of mouth, had discovered the execution of Marcus before Baeck could appeal and succeed in his release. Eventually, Baeck was arrested as well and held in Theresienstadt Ghetto.

Set up to function as propaganda, the ghetto was filmed, photographed, and reported as a thriving small town where elderly Jews could *retire* and younger Jews awaited *work assignments* in the east. However, Theresienstadt was nothing more than ghetto poorly maintained where prisoners were starved and mostly forgotten. Most of the prisoners were transferred to killing centers in Nazi-occupied eastern Germany. The camp was liberated in 1945, and Leo Baeck was found to have survived. Eventually, he joined his daughter in London.

At the confirmation of Marcus's execution at Dachau, Bertha quietly curled up in her leather chair by Robert's bedside and watched him sleep through the night. She had kept Eddy's call from London quiet, and for the time being, to herself. She was grateful to still be in Carl and Freida's house, near family and anchored far away from a life that now seemed surreal. But she shed no tears, felt no pain, and had no answers for potential questions. The moment was hers alone to process.

Thousands of days had passed, thousands of emotions, thoughts, dreams, nightmares, fears, pains, losses—millions of tears. It would be years until Anna's death would be confirmed in records that Bertha would eventually research. Like millions, she simply disappeared into the numbers of camp victims never to be heard of again, only to resurface on ledgers kept at camps that were recorded by the Nazis like battle notches on their belts. Their very existence was reduced to piles of shoes and other trinkets that camp personnel found useless. Photographs of their lives before internment and extermination were clenched in the hands of the few that survived and were left behind.

Carl had survived and returned from the war and bonded quickly with Robert. Together, they tended to chores, a garden, a few farm animals, and Carl's first love—carpentry. Over time, he built a lucrative business. With America's housing boom after the war, Carl's skills and keen talent for precision details and intricate craftsmanship allotted him a respected name in the field. Cabinetry, flooring, hand-carved stair railings, and rich, deep crown moldings were the details new homeowners craved. But his greatest joy was creating beautiful pieces for Freida and Bertha. Tinkering in the special wood shop he had built on the back of their property, Carl and Robert spent many hours in quiet contentment together. Their silent bond was confirmed through each new creation and the sounds of hammering, sanding, and sawing was the only language necessary. Sunday afternoons were reserved for time in the shed, only to be interrupted by a visit from Freida with a small basket of warm *brezel* (soft pretzel) thinly lathered with rich, creamy butter. As Robert grew to his teens, a small stoneware cup of beer was included. The mere waft of the warm *brezel* always made him smile, and the brief savory break from carpentry would become one of his fondest memories with Carl. And, as well, with beer.

Freida took great joy in tending to Robert's every need. Like her husband, she also had a quiet nature and typically only spoke when she deemed necessary. Never able to conceive, she happily embraced the little boy as her own. Although Robert would feel closest to Bertha throughout his life, he grew fond of Freida and loved her for the gentle care she always provided. Together, they shared cooking and gardening.

He grew to love the conversations about the victory gardens during the war and appreciated Freida's dedication to the continuation of growing their own food. Like carpentry, gardening would become his lifelong diversion.

As well, Freida shared many stories and recipes from the days of growing up in the Berlin bakery. She talked frequently about her aunt Ruth and uncle Boris and how much she appreciated, loved, and missed them. Often, when the reference of her aunt and uncle found its way into the conversation, Robert would notice a faraway look in Freida's eyes. Once, he found the courage to ask her where Ruth and Boris had gone. She quietly shook her head and stated that she was confident they were in heaven sharing recipes with friends.

It was years later when Robert surmised that Ruth and Boris had probably succumbed to the same destiny as his biological parents, Marcus and Anna. For him, they all had simply disappeared with little reference, and an imminent silence indicated it to be a taboo subject. He never specifically asked about them again, allowing Freida to share when she felt the need. Unlike Carl, Freida appeared at ease when talking about her and Bertha's life in Berlin together. Carl politely avoided the subject and simply stated that he was "getting too old to remember."

Bertha often reminded Robert that the war was too difficult for many of the soldiers to think about or share. Therefore, they simply chose not to discuss it further. Robert's hesitation to discuss his own parents created a mutually understood silence. Robert did, however, urge Freida to share the stories he enjoyed and knew she would delight in telling of the awful turnip recipes, Bertha's love for chatter with customers, and the delicious smells of fresh baked goods that drew people in from the streets on crisp cool Berlin mornings.

Robert's relationship with Bertha remained strong and close. His lifelong love for her was the closest thing he felt to a real mother. Bertha would joyously state that she and Robert "grew up together."

Although Robert acknowledged Carl and Freida as his parents in their household, his strong bond with Bertha would continue throughout his life. Eventually, Carl and Freida adopted Robert, and he was quite happy for the presence of both father and mother. Like the other boys in the neighborhood, Robert enjoyed being part of a typical American household. But it was his aunt Bertha that he would always ran to when sad, troubled, or needed advice. As well, they continued to enjoy sharing books, film, and history together. She was his sanctuary, and he was hers.

In the beginning, Bertha enjoyed living with Carl and Freida. Moving into the big farmhouse with the beautiful views of green rolling hills reminded her of the time with Richard and their life together in England. In the evening, she would sit in her old leather chair by the window of her bedroom, sip her tea, listen to the radio, and reminisce. When still small enough, Robert would join her by squeezing himself into the chair between Bertha and Bear.

But as time moved on, so did Robert. He created his own evening rituals, many of which were with the other boys in the neighborhood—riding bikes, catching fireflies, whispering about girls. As he gained his independence, Bertha grew tired of her daily routines. She loved her sister and Carl and was grateful to them for taking her and Robert under their wings. Removing herself and Robert from Europe was a gift few had been allowed and she was quite aware of that. But she was far too independent to continue to live in her sister's house. She was becoming anxious and was craving to work again.

Once settled in, Bertha had secured a part-time position with a paper in New York. She wrote mostly from home on a small typewriter in her bedroom when Robert was younger. When articles were ready to submit she took the train into Manhattan. This satisfied Bertha for a while. Quickly, however, she found herself in New York more and more. As Robert gained his independence as a teen, Bertha found New York beckoning her as a rite of passage. At forty-five, she was still a young woman and felt the need for her own life in her own space. Eventually, she secured an apartment and would stay for brief periods at a time. Then finally, she moved there permanently.

Eddy periodically visited Bertha and Robert in New Jersey, and Robert knew him as Uncle Eddy. When Bertha moved to New York, Eddy made the transition permanently as well. But Bertha never stayed away too long. Weekends, holidays, and special occasions always found Bertha back visiting those she loved, especially her best guy, Robert. For Eddy, the door was always open to their home and Eddy was considered family.

When he started driving, Robert would pick her up at the train station. She couldn't help but chuckle when she saw him sitting on the hood of the car waving at the approaching train. She could spot his long lanky arms a mile away, flapping wildly. She was proud of the young man he was becoming. Tall and thin with thick dark curly hair, he was the mirror image of a young Marcus. But Robert was his own personality. He was the perfect combination of Marcus and Richard. She marveled at how one human could take on all the necessary qualities of those who touched their lives and make one perfect being. And to Bertha, Robert was perfect.

In 1967, Robert graduated from Rutgers University with a bachelor's degree in civil engineering. It was at the graduation that Bertha first met Susan Sydel, the pretty young woman Robert would marry two years later. Bertha liked her immediately. She was cordial, gregarious, and smart. Graduating the previous year, she had secured an internship with a prestigious law firm. Bertha and Susan would become great friends throughout the years and shared a lifetime of mutual love and care for Robert. Once graduated, employed, and married, Robert and Susan bought a home not far from Carl and Freida's in Grayson. It was a large older home, closer to town, that needed just the amount of cosmetic care in which Robert could tinker. He was excited about the project and made most of the transformations on his own.

On June 1, 1972, Robert and Susan welcomed their only child, Elijah Paul Henich. He was tiny and precious, with the same full head of dark, curly hair. With the news of their son's birth, Robert and Susan had very little difficulty convincing Bertha to move closer to them in Grayson. At sixty-seven, she had grown tired of the city and had been debating her move for a couple of years. With the inheritance from Richard, Bertha had bought a small but charming apartment in Manhattan years earlier. There, she was happy with her job and friends. She enjoyed a full life of theater, film, music, and walking to outdoor markets.

Although she dated frequently and found herself occasionally involved in short-term romances, abandonment of her freedom was something she couldn't fathom. For Bertha, men were simply a distraction. She kept busy with her continuation of volunteering for area shelters for the homeless and hungry and especially focused on families new to the country in need of jobs and housing. When she eventually retired from her job, save the few articles she voluntarily submitted or edited to community papers, she found herself ready to make another move.

Many of her older friends had passed away, and her younger friends had become busy starting their own families. As well, Eddy had moved to California fifteen years earlier after meeting his lifelong partner, Glenn. The consistent battle for the rights of homosexuals led them to a more liberal state where they felt more freedom. Although the struggles continued, there were large pockets of California that afforded better housing and championed for more supportive legislation. As well, they both loved the beach and warmer weather while Eddy continued his career working for small nonprofit newspapers that allowed him to use his voice.

Although Bertha had made several visits to Eddy, she found herself more content when closer to home as she got older. Her difficulty with walking and running as a child eventually intensified with age, provoking her to become dependent on a cane for long periods of standing or walking. So, for a hefty profit, she sold her apartment, packed up her cat, and surprised the whole family when she purchased a large craftsman-style home in Grayson, a mere five blocks from Robert and Susan. Ignoring the family's concern for a large house with stairs and living alone, Bertha asserted her usual independence and politely refused the many offers of living with anyone. As she did most of her life, she embraced the challenges as a way of securing her longevity. She refused to become sedentary or dependent regardless of any difficulty. Although Robert was more than happy to renovate or fix anything for her, she declined most of the offers only to accept the necessary attention to leaky faucets, broken stair steps, and so on. She loved the old creaky house just as it was and often stated that it reminded her of her *beginnings*.

Over time, Bertha enjoyed watching Eli grow, learn to walk, talk, play. They would never experience the same closeness that she and Robert had enjoyed. For little Eli, the age difference was too great, and he would simply see Bertha as an elder...too fragile to completely engage. Her cane was foreign to him and he appeared too shy of getting too close. But for Bertha and Robert, Eli was another miraculous bond they would treasure together. Robert knew how much she loved Eli and, therefore, ensured that she saw him as often as she liked. Bertha was a permanent fixture in their lives, attending school events, soccer games, holidays, and Sunday dinners. And Robert never questioned the occasional calls for help, dropping anything and everything to tend to her needs. Although their lives became routine, much like everyone else, their family would cling to the special silent camaraderie of a shared past.

The trauma and invisible scars of history drifted away with those who experienced the worst of it. The love and attention of Bertha's generation paved the way for new generations to flourish. What had once cut to the very core, eventually mended but was never forgotten.

School children continued to learn of the Holocaust in their textbooks, with careful attention to the statistics, dates, and memorizing sequential events of the war. But the real stories, the heart of the true loss, endurance, and ultimate survival of a culture, religion, race, would be protected in the personal intimate stories so difficult to retell.

Some passed stories on to their children and grandchildren through scrapbooks and photo albums—documents that would carry on the true lineage of an entire population that refused to be broken. The single image of Robert's parents had been secured in Bertha's scrapbook. And someday, Eli would inherit Bertha's set of intimate stories, all meticulously saved in her journal. Saved in a large coat box, preserved and treasured throughout the years in a musty attic, carefully preserved photos and documents would fill some of the gaps of his own ancestry, perhaps answering his many curious questions of those he loved, and of some he never met.

22

He allowed himself to be swayed by his conviction
that human beings are not born once and for all
on the day their mothers give birth to them,
but that life obliges them
over and over again
to give birth to themselves.
—Gabriel García Márquez, *Love in the Time of Cholera*

*M*EGAN RACHAEL HENICH.
I had counted all the *H*s in line. She was eleventh and the only Henich. Still, I jumped, startled at hearing my own child's name. As she walked across the stage, my emotions got away from me. I could feel the tears start to well up, the throat close, the embarrassment of a grown man sobbing at his daughter's high school graduation. She was stunning, sophisticated, smart, confident—everything I felt I had not been in high school. I was convinced that my child stood out. I'm sure most parents in the audience felt the exact same way about their children. But in my heart, I knew Meg was special. I knew she'd come from a long line of really fucking special.

Principal Moore handed her the diploma, shook her hand. She moved the gold tassel to the other side of the mortarboard, slightly turned, caught my eye, and winked. That did it. It was over in a flash.

It was all too quick. Every damn bit of it—from birth to now. And now, she was off to college.

I started to hyperventilate. Penny knew me all too well and put her arm around my shoulder to console me. Mom was missing. I quickly scanned the crowd but didn't see her. She'd stated that she needed to go to the bathroom as soon as we sat down. I was sure she stopped and talked to everyone along the way.

And just how a ten-year-old would act, Robby pointed at me while I was frantically wiping my wet face on my shirt, and burst into laughter. He had Penny's smile, freckles, and crystal-blue eyes. But his features were Dad's, and his contagious laugh was Mom's. I typically found it difficult to be angry with him.

When Penny and I got married, the conversation of children had never surfaced. I admit that I slightly avoided the subject. But I couldn't help noticing Penny's delight when receiving an invite to a friend's baby shower. Her attention to detail in each gift was above and beyond. The invites were slapped on the fridge held by a magnet of a small gold replica of the Eiffel Tour, the only souvenir we could afford on our honeymoon to Europe.

She couldn't stop talking about everyone else's babies and all their milestones. It was on our first anniversary that the conversation took the turn. I asked Mom to help with the perfect gift, and she emailed me immediately. Evidently, the first anniversary is tradi-tionally paper. *Paper? What the hell?* But the modern version went with a clock or time. Since letter writing had been replaced with texting, stationery was no longer a gift for the new millennium. So I got her a book of romantic poetry, and Mom insisted I give her a watch that had been Bertha's.

No one knew the watch's origins, but none of us could remember her without it, either. I felt it was a little antiquated and was unsure how Penny would react. She loved Bertie, but Penny was modern, no frills, minimalistic. The small ornate silver face was encrusted with tiny diamonds held together with a delicate small black satin strap. I took Mom's advice on this one, got it cleaned and working again, and wrapped it up. All the bases were covered, paper and time.

We went out for dinner, drank wine, talked, and laughed. It was what we did best. I could get lost in Penny, and the rest of the world just melted away. She was my best friend and my best lover. When she opened her gifts, she cooed and giggled. I was proud she liked the poetry book. And she appeared grateful to have something of Bertie's. For a moment, she ran her fingers across the watch, all the while smiling. I had to admit it looked beautiful on her thin tan wrist. Then came the bomb.

"Speaking of time ticking." She sheepishly batted her eyelashes. I knew it. I knew it would eventually come to this. I wasn't interested in more children. I was deliriously happy, and Meg had turned out perfect. I didn't want to push that envelope. But I was deeply in love with her and to deny Penny the joy I had felt with a child was selfish.

Damn, I should have just stuck with paper! If she was going to announce a pregnancy, then there wasn't going to be anything standing in the way of pure joy. I took a deep breath and waited for the announcement. She wasn't pregnant yet, but she *would like to be!* I was relieved. *Breathe in…breathe out.* But as the evening progressed, the wine, the necking in the back of the cab, the hot tub, nine months later, we welcomed a baby boy into our lives. Meg was thrilled.

As an eight-year-old, he was a living doll that she could cuddle and dress. We named him Robert Marcus Henich—Robbie, for short. Mom was delighted and wept when she heard the name choice.

Dad was my father, and Carl was my grandfather. I didn't really embrace any others. But knowing the true story of Bertha, Marcus, Anna, all of them, connected me and throughout my life answered questions and helped me make sense of my world. I felt Robby and Meg had a right to that connection as well.

On our honeymoon, we toured Germany, England, and France. Certainly, some of the highlights were places I had read and imagined in Bertha's journal. We stayed in the Hufeisensiedlung Apartments, Bertha's first solo home. Some of the units had been accommodated as rentals for tourists. It was one of my favorite stops. We were able to rent an apartment for a couple of days. It had been upgraded since the 1930s of course, but some of the features remained. I spent all night staring at the fire in the old refurbished corner wood stove envisioning Aunt Bertha as a young woman, excited and full of promise.

As well, we went to Richard's estate in England. Now a bed-and-breakfast, we were able to walk through the cozy rooms, stare out the windows, and love the very hills and green pastures Bertha had so beautifully described. It was at that moment I realized the powerful connections. With my wife and two children, I was living in the New Jersey house that Richard's funds had provided for Bertha. He wouldn't get to see that house, and I wouldn't get to meet him. But I was confident he knew the importance of his inheritance to her and Dad.

I knew that somehow he envisioned his single stone creating ripples in the water, one right after another, all connected and yet creating their individual rings. Evidently, he knew she was smart and strong, and he was confident she'd use the money wisely. He knew she'd take care of the little boy they had all grown to love and forever become his family. And she had. These were her milestones. Milestones she continued to cross regardless of the heinous surroundings, the pain, the loss. When finished she handed them to Robert. And then to me. They were the silent gift that connected us and helped us all to find our way.

Unlike many tourists of Jewish heritage, I opted out of visiting any of the concentration camps or Holocaust museums. Not only was I on my honeymoon and chose not to carry those visions into the bridal suite, I preferred to revisit the life given instead. I already knew how people died. I wanted to know how, in the worst of circumstances, they continued to live.

It dawned on me that Bertha had known Penny and loved her—as a neighbor, a friend, and perhaps a confidante when it came to matters of the heart. *Girl talk*, Penny called it. And respectfully, Penny kept those secret liaisons of Bertha's to herself. For that I was eternally grateful. But I knew Aunt Bertha would be delighted to know that Penny was now part of my milestones. And Bertha's wristwatch was merely a symbol of our brief moments on this earth and how we all found each other void of common space and time.

My thoughts were interrupted with the eruption of applause and a standing ovation. Graduation was over, and I'd missed the governor's speech. *Thank God!* Mom had found her way back to her seat. She was giggly, energetic, and sweaty. I took her elbow and guided her out, ensuring I could get her to the car and some bottled water.

Sitting at the long table in the restaurant, it was possible that I was drifting in and out of my past to avoid the pomp and circumstance Natalie had arranged for the graduation dinner. She sat at the end of the table as if the event was in her honor. She was flanked on one side by her new husband, Patrick. I didn't have much of an opinion of him as we rarely connected. A quick *hello* or *how are you?* on the phone was all we ever exchanged. Once married to others, Natalie and I moved on with our lives and paid little attention to each other. We had become polite strangers.

Patrick was personable and somewhat quiet, poor sap. I often wondered if he had regrets. But truthfully, he seemed happy and appeared to enjoy catering to her every whim. As well, to avoid uncomfortable forced conversation, Patrick quickly shoved a beer in my hands, and for that alone, I secretly liked the guy.

Natalie was flanked on the other side by a woman named Regina. One of Natalie's wealthy clients, she was obsessed with decorating her home and had the money to do so, over and over again. This created a cash cow for Natalie. In return, Natalie treated Regina as royalty, creating a toxic superficial reciprocity. To all of us, Regina was simply a tolerated stranger sitting at the table.

Penny, Robby, Mom, and I sat at the other end of the table, most probably a cushy and conveniently planned seating arrangement by Natalie. Meg sat in the center with a young man named Josh. They had met in the school library and had been dating their entire senior year. She had chosen journalism as her preference for Rutgers. I shouldn't have been too surprised as she was fascinated with her great-great-aunt Bertha's stories and had neatly tucked away all of Bertha's memorabilia under her bed for safe keeping. And I had kept every little book Meg had written and illustrated since she was four, convinced that someday she would be a great writer. Josh was headed to Rutgers, too. His track was graphic design. I wondered if the relationship would last once in college. I would be lying if I said I wasn't a little jealous. But he was a nice young man, handsome and smart. I wasn't too surprised at that choice, either.

And there she was, grown up and ready to set sail. That night, I watched her every move, answering questions about college in the fall, course choices, dorms, scholarships. High school is bullshit but just as much a milestone for your child as kindergarten. Certainly, the milestones will appear bigger and better as the years come and go—college, graduation, grad school, first job, marriage, and so on. It never ends. But for the parents watching, each one is an absolute miracle.

Watching her, I thought about that night my mother and I spent in the attic. I thought of those who'd missed out on their children's events. Their milestones had been elevated to things relating to survival alone—food, shelter, escape trains, concentration camps. I couldn't stop thinking about Bertha, Carl, and Freida, and of course, Dad. I was wishing they were all here. And somehow, I knew they were. They were obviously present in the faces of my children. I wanted them to see that their pain, suffering, and sacrifice was not been forgotten and the important role they played in our lives. I wanted to include Marcus and Anna in the invites, send them photos, and thank them. If not for them, I wouldn't have what I have, and I wouldn't be here. And that was just unthinkable.

I loved my children and wife to the very core of my soul. I couldn't image putting them on a train and sending them off to a life without me. I realized that my own selfish thoughts were, indeed, a milestone, one of which I could revel in the fact that, somehow, we'd all made it to this table together. We were some of the lucky few in this world who didn't have to make such unfathomable choices. Our hearts and lives had not been put to the same tests as our ancestors had endured, and I would be eternally grateful.

The summer was great. We spent time traveling about locally, in and out of small towns, antique stores, and restaurants. A splurge at the lake in a cabin was my favorite. Paddle boarding, hiking, and playing with new cameras, just hanging around. Ending the day with wine, movies, board games, and more wine. And the firepit chats under the stars was the best. I was soaking up every moment I could with Meg. We invited Josh to join us and it turned out to be a good call. However, I accommodated him in a room down the hall opposite Meg with my room in between, of course. Getting to know him better helped to remind me that Meg was the smart one, the one that made good choices. She was strong and focused, and her decision-making skills far exceeded anyone else, especially mine. Josh was a great guy and, for now, I approved.

Three months after Meg's graduation, I flew to California to visit Eddy. He was the only human being still alive that knew Bertha during her entire adult life, from a joyous young woman, still discovering her ambition in journalism and love, to a happily settled urban American-Jew embracing friends, family, and all that the art world had to offer. My grandmother's dementia had grabbed and stolen her memory and she no longer proved to be a reliable source. Hopeful Eddy was still cognitively alive, I lucked out.

Eddy was a remarkable ninety-nine-year-old living in an assisted-living apartment in San Francisco. His lifelong partner had died twenty-seven years earlier, but photos of Glenn were everywhere in the small efficient room. Not at all what I was expecting, he was still cognitively sharp and extremely personable. Restricted to a wheelchair, he leaned forward to shake my hand.

"Are you my nursing attendant for the day?" he smiled.

"No. Bertha Plesser was my great-aunt. I hope I haven't—"

"Oh, my stars!" he exclaimed. "Are you Robert's boy?" he yelled. "Eli! How wonderful!"

We sat and talked for hours. Next to my mother, I do believe he was the most joyous human I have ever met. He had an amazing sense of humor and was a great storyteller. He had retained his British accent and was able to cleverly manipulate his words with a quick wit. For the first time, I could picture Bertha as a young woman, laughing, storytelling, running around London and New York, writing. I was totally engaged by his presence, and it was clearly obvious why Bertha and Dad loved him so much.

"I loved your dad. He belonged to us all! And I miss Bertie!" he exclaimed. "She was quite a woman! I envied her! So smart and strong. She was like a big sister to me. She understood me when no one else appeared to *get it*, if you know what I mean. And the cutest little button you have ever seen! She wasn't much for fashion—you know, too German!" He threw his head back and howled with laughter.

"And when she fell for a guy, she fell hard!" he added. "But she always bounced right back up! 'Screw them!' she would yell. She just kept busy. But little Robert, now that was her real love! As for the others, well, they just came and went." He rolled his eyes and sat back in the pillow-cushioned chair.

Some awkward silence deafened the room. I didn't want to interfere in what appeared to be a personal moment of reminiscing. From reading Bertha's journal, I was very aware of her connection with Marcus. I could handle reading it alone but discussing it out loud was a different story.

Eddy stared around the room, and finally, with a softer voice, he said, "Not me. When I fell hard I just stayed down there. I lucked out when I met Glenn. It was a hot steamy day at Venice Beach, and everyone was trying to out muscle each other." He grinned. "But not my Glenny. There he was, tan and lean, stretched out on a towel under a giant umbrella, reading Ginsberg's *Howl*!" He emphasized the word with an animated smirk.

"He was brilliant. He started out writing and editing for ONE Magazine in 1953," he continued to brag. "It was one of the only magazines in the country dedicated to the homosexual community. It's first cover was *Homosexual Marriages*!" He swooped his hand high across the room as he announced the title, placing it in the lights of a virtual marquee. "Can you imagine?" He laughed. "My Glenny would be so proud in this new millennium. And we'd be married!" He laughed and laughed.

Eventually, I could see he was running out of steam. His eyes struggled with the weight of his eyelids. He held on a little longer through several typical questions about me, my career, wife, children, and so on. There really wasn't much more to say. My life, and those in it, were just the result of all the people he knew and loved. But they were gone now.

I stood up and grabbed my keys to the rental car. It caught his attention, and he blurted, "Hold on a minute. Get in the top drawer of that little table over there, dear boy." He pointed across the room. "There's a small blue picture book. Bring it to me."

Eddy slowly turned page after page studying the photos pasted in the book. Occasionally, he would thumb through a loose stack that never made it into a permanent spot.

"Ah!" he finally exclaimed. "Here. Take this one. Aside from raising Robert, here's the other job she really loved!" I took the photo. Bertha was sitting at an old desk with a typewriter in a large room of what looked like hundreds of other people working. She looked like a child, about the same age as Meg. She was leaning back in a chair waving at the camera with both hands in the air and flashing a big smile.

Cute as a button, indeed.

"Take it!" Eddy insisted. "It would make her happy for you to have it. Maybe that smart daughter of yours will be inspired by her!" He laughed out loud again.

The flight from LA to Newark was long, late, and crowded. I was wedged in a window seat and relished the fact that I could stare out the window into the dark and ignore the others that had been crammed in next to me like sardines. I was getting crabby and wasn't looking forward to baggage claim. I took the picture of Bertha out of my wallet and stared at it again. It made me smile. I flipped it over. On the back was some faded script, handwritten, probably by Bertha. It matched the script from her journal. But then again, that was the script of the past. It was that beautiful longhand that had eventually become a lost art when our world was invaded by technology. It was hard to see so I clicked on the small overhead beam allotted as a reading lamp in the dark fuselage. The guy next to me flinched, and I could see in my peripheral vision he was pissed. Served him right for hoarding the armrest. I slightly smirked to myself as I put on my glasses.

Bertie, 1941, London

I took another look at the photo and studied the details. I was jolted by an unexpected air pocket followed by a roller coaster of turbulence. *Damn it! Breathe in…breathe out.* Eventually, it smoothed out, and the pilot apologized over the speaker. I started to relax again and secured the photo back into my wallet for safe keeping, turned off the light, and continued to stare into darkness. I felt calm and content. I was happy. I was grateful for the discovery of Bertha's life, my father's journey, his parent's sacrifice, and my grandparent's love. I missed my wife and children and was anxious to tell them of my trip and of Eddy. I was happy, and I was going home.